*From reviews of Troy Blacklaw's first novel,* Karoo Boy

'*Karoo Boy* is the most colourful book I have ever read.'
– Chris Martin, singer of the band Coldplay

'A beautifully evocative coming-of-age story of life in
South Africa.' – Bryce Courtenay

'Blacklaws conveys all the horrors of apartheid without being
overt or didactic: he simply, lyrically, captures truth. Such is
the charm of his prose, it produces that Nabokovian tingle in
the spine.' – Zulfikar Ghose

'This story is set out in prose honed by a writer with an unusually
keen ability to make words yield their music.'
– Denis Hirson, author of *I Remember King Kong (The Boxer)*

'It is not often that a book demands to be devoured with gusto
as the plot ebbs and flows through effortless prose …'
– *Daily Dispatch*, South Africa

'*Karoo Boy* is so effortless and yet so laden.' – Johan Myburg,
South African journalist and poet

'His language is as rich as the sea smell which is lodged in Douglas'
being, and his understanding of the universal loneliness often felt by
teenagers is raw and tender.' – *Natal Mercury*

'*Karoo Boy* is beautifully written and hauntingly evocative,
a South African version of *The Catcher in the Rye* perhaps.'
– *Sunday Independent*, Johannesburg

# Blood Orange

# BLOOD ORANGE

by

Troy Blacklaws

DOUBLE
STOREY
a juta company

*The author's earnings from the sale of the book in South Africa will go to a street shelter in Cape Town.*

First published 2005 in southern Africa by
Double Storey Books, a division of Juta & Co. Ltd,
Mercury Crescent, Wetton, Cape Town

ISBN 1-919930-96-5

Page layout by Claudine Willatt-Bate
Cover design by Michiel Botha
Cover photos by Troy Blacklaws
Printing by Paarl Print, Paarl

*For Daniela*

## Foreword

*Blood Orange* by Troy Blacklaws is a vivid testament to a white teenager's torments and trials in an apartheid society which tries to impose on him privileges and perceptions he rejects as unearned and unjust.

It is episodic and disconnected in style, the author using this device to depict adolescence as the fragmented gathering of sometimes unrelated perceptions in his unsophisticated transition through his teens.

Yet there is an overarching sweep to it, because it is set against a backdrop of South Africa in all its geographic variety and scenic impact, and its cameos are all jigsaw pieces in this overall puzzle so recognisable to South Africans as the authentic whole of their national experience. In other words, you do not have to be a particular type of South African, nor specifically black nor white, to recognise the essential familiarity of these jigsaw pieces.

And you don't even have to be South African to acknowledge the power and validity of this particular treatment of youth, since so many of the doubts, fears, hopes and insights the writer details are universal.

Donald Woods
London, 1998

## Thanks to

Daniela, who loved this story through all the sketches and drafts. Finn-Christian, who begged me time and again to tell of Africa in this far, foreign place. Mia, for whom Africa is guineafowl feathers and Zulu beads. My folks for the vivid palette of my boyhood. My play shadow, Dean. The Heramb boys and Jabuz for the neverending games of cricket under the pines. James Scorer, Finn Spicer, Francois Tredoux for proofreading. Gillian Warren-Brown, Andrew Stooke, Sioux Damerell, Nantume Makumbi for their wise tips. Fish and the boys of Platoon 10. Zane Godwin, Peter Watson, Neil Wetmore and Johan Myburg for firing my dreaming in East London. Nigel and Alison Gwynne-Evans for giving me refuge in London. Caryn Edwards, David Grunberg, Meg Forster, Fréro Francois, Himali Upadhya and Andi Hänssig for their passion. Olivia Rose-Innes for honing my words. Russell Martin for his tuned eye. Isobel Dixon for her skill and soul. Meneer Coetzer and Mister Slater, teachers at Paarl Boys' High, who gave me a sense of the world beyond the blackboard. Their voices still echo in my head. Delarey, wherever you are, for the free pints under a bitter moon. My students, who endured readings of the novel as it unravelled.

# Blood Orange

# Zulu juju

Natal is the land of the Zulus. Hills dotted with cows and clay huts run from the Drakensberg down to the sea, where bananas, pawpaws and palms tangle on the sand and sharks glide in the deep.

I am called Gecko, for as a tot I gurgled with glee at the sight of the rubbery, magic-fingered lizards on the roof over my cot. I am seven and my brother Zane is just three. He is named after Zane Grey, writer of the cowboy paperbacks my father reads. Zane has the blue eyes of my father, the jeep-riding, cow-herding farmer. I have the olive-green eyes of my mother who was a nurse in Addington Hospital in Durban. Now she is just a mother out on the farm, far from the flicker of dizzy lights and the whistles of the barefoot rickshawmen.

Beauty is our Zulu nanny. She calls Zane and me *white Zulus* for our feet are hard from barefoot running and we love to mouth Zulu words. When she rolls her rolling pin, her fat jellies and she sings a Zulu song, sad as black bass weaving through reeds. Sometimes Zane and I and Beauty's boy Jamani drop our lizard chasing and bird hunting just to listen to her river song. When I was still a piccanin she tutuzela'd me on her back, a back-to-front kangaroo. Snug in the hollow of her back, I felt her humming and singing seep into me.

Beauty loves sweets: luckydip sweets, lollipops, jellytots, the lot. She sniffs out our hidden sweets and blames it on the rats. The other thing Beauty loves is seawater. We bring back Coca-Cola bottles of seawater from Chaka's Rock, where we caravan under palms in which monkeys chitter and chase. Beauty believes the seawater is magic. At sunrise, when the nkankaan bird cries *ha ha haaa,* she drinks a bitter swig of Indian Ocean and it makes her feel good and strong. My father says that it is all the swiped sweets that make her strong.

At dusk Beauty comes out to catch Zane and me for our bath, the dogs, Dingaan and Dingo, yapping at her heels. I dart off and hide in the hibiscus jungle. Zane ropeladders up the old jacaranda tree and Beauty has to lure him down with the bribe of a ride on her back. Then Beauty comes after me, with Zane clinging to her like a beady-eyed nagapie.

Jonas, the old man gardenboy who haunts the shadows of our backyard, giggles toothlessly at us and rolls a cigarette out of newspaper and Boxer tobacco. Owls swoop in the dusk and Cape turtledoves call *karoo karoo* in the bluegums.

Beauty catches me in the end and squeezes me against her watermelon bubs. So it is that hippos kill more men in Africa than lions do. With a lion you are always on edge, for it may just chase if it is hungry. With a hippo you laugh as it plods in the mud. Then, before you can say Pietermaritzburg, it charges and it's bye-bye blackbird.

Cooped in the tub, Beauty scrubs us till our skin tingles. One time she swatted me on my bare bum because I stood on the edge of the tub and peed down onto Zane's head. Her swat stung like blazes. Still, Zane and I play monkey tricks on her. We splash her, so her pink pinafore looks like a map of the world with damp seas and dry land. We pull the doek off her head, and her spongy hair springs up free.

Whenever she baths her Jamani in the tin tub in the rondavel hut in our backyard, she Vaselines his skin until it gleams. Though I beg her to Vaseline us, she just rubs Zane and me dry with towels until it feels as if our skin will snakeskin off. While she dries us she jams her hips against the door in case we bolt barebum into the yard again. Jamani (in my tatty hand-me-down shorts) peeps at us from the door. He laughs at our larks but he never jumps into the tub with us. Beauty forbids him to but she will not tell me why.

Lucky Strike is our Zulu cook. He tells Zane and me stories while we eat our supper in the kitchen. Beauty and Jamani stay to listen for a while before going outside to their rondavel. Lucky Strike tells us how the warriors of Chaka, the Zulu king, ran barefoot over duwweltjies to prove their manhood. He tells us how the sangoma in leopard skins and cow tails reads the future in scattered bones, stones and cowrie shells. How he breathes over the bones to witch Xhosa enemies into porcupines or tortoises.

While his voice flows, Lucky Strike juggles hissing pots and smoking pans on the iron stove that gobbles up bluegum wood.

⌒

On holidays we eat at the long table in the dining-room with my mother and father and the zebra skin on the wall. My father tells us how he shot the zebra, and of the time he shot two springbok with one bullet. By fluke the bullet flew through the head of one buck and felled another running behind. My mother *tut tuts*. Zane and I beg him to go on telling, but he wants to hear the BBC news on the radio. He has a deep lion's voice and when he goes *tula*, Zane and I tula.

The BBC tells us there is a star called Ringo in England. Ringo rhymes with our dog Dingo.

My father is my hero. He is strong and carries me up high on his shoulders so I can see over the heads at tombola fairs in Howick. My father taught me how to thread an earthworm onto a hook to catch bass, to curve a cricket ball in the air, to carve a cattie out of a forked stick to shoot starlings – ratty black birds that glint hints of green and pink in the sun.

Once a fluke tennis ball flew from his racquet to kill a swooping bat.

My father, like a hardy cowboy, does not cry. One time he had his foot inside a gumboot when the lawnmower blade took the tip off his big toe. My mother bound his toe in cloth she tore from his shirt to dry the blood. My father chirped: Hey, Nurse, ever had a fling with a farmer? My mother frowned: You think you're Gary Cooper.

To me my father is Gary Cooper in *High Noon*. If he says *jump*, I jump. If he says *tula*, I tula. And if there is one thing that riles him, it is when I do not eat my peas. If I could I'd gulp them down just to see him smile at me, his skebenga, his rascal, but when I swallow a soggy, rabbitpoo pea I have to jam my teeth to keep all my food from flying up out of me.

I stare hard at my peas and mutter a juju: kudu, Zulu, kangaroo, Timbuktu. But the peas will not be witched away to Timbuktu. My father always growls: Think of all the starving kids in Biafra. I never see how eating up all my peas helps the kids in Biafra. I want to tell my father to send my peas to Biafra. My father makes me stay at the table till all my peas are gone. This gives me time to think about all the starving kids in Biafra. Their fathers are too poor to shoot springbok or zebra, so they never eat meat.

I sit all alone and sulk over my peas. Lucky Strike undecks the table, but does not dare touch my cursed china. Lucky Strike clicks his tongue, as if to say: Fool boy to be caged in while your brother plays in the yard. I beg him for a pea juju, one that will turn the peas into pink luckydip sweets, but he just goes: Aikona, young baas, the magic is not for such small things.

Sometimes I drop my peas on the floor, hoping Dingaan and Dingo will gobble them up, but they just lick them and sniff at them. When my mother cooks butternut and peas I hollow out the butternut skin and tip it over to hide the peas underneath. A tortoise full of bitter green eggs. Although my mother knows, she never tells on me.

1969. A man has landed on the moon. We all go outside to look. On the veranda my father lifts me up onto his shoulders. There is the moon. A scoop of vanilla ice-cream in the sky. My father holds my mother's hand as if they know the American up there and are scared he will fall. Zane is fooling around with Dingaan and Dingo. I look long and hard but I see no man on the moon, just a fuzzy, rabbity smudge.

– I think he is on the other side, my mother whispers.

This is a pity. I have never seen a live yankee-doodle dandy, just flick heroes like Clint Eastwood.

– The world will never be the same again, my father says.

I have hardly discovered the world as it is, and already it is changing. What amazes me more than a man on the moon is a voice coming over the radio all the way from America, for you can see the moon with your bare eyes but you cannot see America even from the top of the Drakensberg.

After supper Zane and I always lie on the veranda and rest our heads against the matted and blackjacked hair of the dogs and listen to Springbok Radio with my mother and father. I am glad, whenever there is a murder on the radio, that we do not have TV in South Africa. The sight of blood and guts oozing out of a bullet hole would give me nightmares.

My father reads *The Natal Mercury* with his dusty boots up. You can smell the dust, the smoke from his Texans, his sweat from being out under the sun all day. After he's read the paper he picks up a Zane Grey. He unfolds a folded corner and he's gone.

My mother loves her bare, hard-skinned heels tickled and reads fat books with no drawings about the moon and the stars while the radio chats and the crickets chirp.

– Your life is all mapped out in the stars, my mother sometimes tells me.

I gawp at the moon and the stars: a scattering of white bones and shells thrown by a sangoma in the sky. I hope I will hear the whisper of his breath telling my future.

Is it in my blood to go overseas? Will I ever go as far from Natal as America? How will I die? Will I be jawed by a tiger shark? Or be bitten by a black mamba and jitter to death? Will I die in a motorcar, like James Dean? (Torn out of *The Natal Mercury* he lies inside my mother's Bible, among photographs and dry palm crosses.)

I see no man on the moon. I hear no sangoma in the sky. If they are out there, they are playing hide-and-seek.

⁓

At bedtime we pray to God with my mother, while my father stands in the doorway. Though we pray in the Christian way, I picture God as an old, white-haired sangoma in raggedy leopard skins, an assegai in one hand, a handful of rattling bones in the other. My mother says I am free to picture God as a Zulu if I want to, but I should not tell at school.

Zane and I murmur: God bless my brother, mother and father, grandmothers and grandfathers, Beauty and Jamani, Lucky Strike, Jonas, Dingaan and Dingo, my horse Tomtom. Chase away the mamba and the evil men. Amen.

The evil men are out there in the dark. They come from the north with pangas and guns. You do not see them in the dark. They kill old men and women in faraway farm houses. They burn things. They blow things up. I am glad my father has a shotgun to shoot the evil men, if they come. I sleep with my Swiss Army knife under my pillow. You never know if God has a gecko's eye on us, or if he is dreaming.

The only animal we do not pray for is old Amos, a beak-headed tortoise the size of a wine box. Lucky Strike told us he was once a Xhosa warrior, witched into a tortoise by a Zulu sangoma a hundred years ago. Zane and I ride him or stand tiptoe on his shell to pluck down high mangoes and bananas. I wonder whether he will ever be witched back into a Xhosa warrior. If so, would he know the things Amos has seen, or would he be dazed by a world of Chevs, radios, cinemas and aeroplanes?

We do not pray for Amos because we do not tangle with Zulu juju.

When I peek through my fingers, I see my father standing there, his eyes open. If he catches me peeking, he winks at me. Afterwards, my mother bends down and kisses us on the forehead. I breathe in her sweet jasmine smell. Then my father turns out the light with the Zulu words for *see you tomorrow*: Bona wena kosasa.

Then Zane and I are alone in the dark. We hear the choir of

crickets and the murmur of Springbok Radio and the whimper of the dogs. They whimper in their doggy dreams of sinking their teeth into the guineafowl and moles that got away.

In the dark Zane spits out his dummy to nag me:

– Joo love Momandaddy?

My love seesaws. I hate my father when he growls at me for not eating my peas, or when he gives me a stinging hiding. I love him when he carries me high on his shoulders, or smokes his Texans with his boots up and ruffles my hair, calling me his little skebenga. I love my mother when she tells of the stars and God and other faraway things. I hate her when she locks me in the pantry till my father comes home, as she did when I cut off all her agapanthus flowers with my Swiss Army knife. She sat there among the blue flowers with her feet folded under her like a Chinese monk and cried: my poor love-flowers, my poor love-flowers. Then she locked me up in the pantry with the high-up window.

In the pantry I watch zizzing flies die on gooey fly paper. I keep my bare feet up on a chair for fear of frogs hiding in the cool shadows among my father's beer bottles.

Grandpa Barter gave me the pocket knife. He said I should not tell anyone but he once saved a Siamese princess from a tiger with the knife. As I lie in bed I gingerly finger the blade. One day I too will be a hero. Though there are no tigers in South Africa, maybe a lion will do. I may have to go to England to find a princess to rescue, but in England there are no tigers or lions to kill. And then there is my mother: she has this thing about hurting flowers and birds and playing with knives or guns. So, Zane and I kill frogs and birds with catties instead.

Another thing Zane wants to know is:

– If you got witched, which animal would you be?

– A kangaroo.

Zane giggles at the thought of the Zulus going *awuuu awuuu* at the sight of a kangaroo in Africa.

– Okay, a cheetah.

– Why?

– Coz then I would run fast as the wind.

Or a dolphin, for then I would swim far out to sea and not be scared of sharks. Or the piet-my-vrou bird, the pezukomkono, and fly from the cold July to the fever sun of Abyssinia in the far north. Or a swift and fly further still, to England to see the circus clowns and dancing bears at Piccadilly. To see the Beefeaters and the bearskin hats of the soldiers guarding the queen.

Zane never wants to be anything but a monkey. I tell him over and over that leopards kill monkeys, but that does not bother him. A monkey is the animal he would be, if a Zulu sangoma witched him.

– What things do you love? Zane whispers.

I love the green juice of the Panado muti my mother gives me when I have a cold. I love the potato chips Lucky Strike cooks. I love the ghostbreath candyfloss you find at tombola fairs. I love to curl up like a cat and fall asleep in the wicker washbasket. I love to watch guyfox fireworks flower the sky from up there on my father's shoulders.

– I love banana ice-cream, chirps Zane.

When we go to the Durban beachfront, where the Zulu rickshawmen kick their feet up high into the sky, the watercolour paintbox of ice-creams always dazes me: granadilla and lemon and vanilla and strawberry and banana and lichi and all sorts.

Zane picks banana and banana and banana. Every time. All

three scoops. You love banana like a bloody monkey, my father laughs. As for me, I always feel my life hangs on the choice. I'll have lemon and vanilla. No no, wait. Lemon and maybe lichi, and or maybe banana and … He'll have lemon, lichi and strawberry, my father tells the ice-cream man. I hate strawberry ice-cream, but it is too late. The strawberry bleeds pink globs into the lemon and lichi, and no Zulu juju can unmix the colours.

# black mamba

Tomtom is my old, moth-eaten horse. Lucky Strike found him wandering in the hills and caught him for me. Tomtom loves to chew grannysmith apples out of my hand with his lazy, tea-coloured teeth. Lucky Strike taught me to ride him bareback and I ride old Tomtom everywhere: down to the likkewaan river and to the polo club. Sometimes I ride to the Karkloof falls, where sad men jump. Tomtom coolly grazes the wet grass at the edge. He is not scared. Just mambas and monkeys spook him.

I gaze down as the mist kisses my face and wonder how sad you have to be to jump:

down down down

dead.

Lucky Strike told me Chaka used to fling his wives down from Chaka's Rock.

In my dreams sharks tug unwanted wives off the rocks. Blood sifts into the water, like tea seeping from a tea-bag.

On the veranda in the evenings, I love to hear the sound of Tomtom snorting and shuffling to and fro. It is good to know he is out there, just beyond the glow of the gas lamp.

When the vervet monkeys come down from the hills Tomtom whinnies and paws the dust. The monkeys dart into the mealie field next to Tomtom's paddock to steal mealie cobs. Tomtom gallops up and down along the fence. The monkeys pick a cob and stick it under one arm and then pick another and try to stick it under, but the first cob drops out. So they pick another and drop another, until my father runs down, swinging the gas lamp, yelling *voetsak voetsak*.

Dingaan and Dingo are scared of the monkeys. They do not run down to the mealie field, but bark from the veranda. The cob-robbers voetsak, a furry flurry, scattering mealies for Lucky Strike to gather and cook for supper tomorrow.

For a long time after the monkeys voetsak, Tomtom is restless.

My mother comes into the kitchen while Lucky Strike cooks mealie cobs.

– Lucky, she teases, you shouldn't run around with all the young Zulu girls.

Lucky Strike laughs and shakes his head.

– Aai aai, Madam.

– How will you fork out lobola cows for them all?

– Aai aai, Madam, he laughs.

He dunks his head into a deep enamel pot.

I love it when my mother comes into the kitchen to tease Lucky Strike, for it puts him in a good mood and he melts Peel's honey in our milk. I wonder where Lucky Strike and all the young Zulu girls run around to. No one tells me. It seems to me that all the world is playing hide-and-seek.

Tomtom lies down, blowing hot wind through his nostrils. He will not get to his feet. I run up to the house for a grannysmith apple and tell Lucky Strike that Tomtom is sick.

– Tomtom is old, young baas. Maybe it is his time, says Lucky Strike, handing me an apple.

The apple slips from Tomtom's foamy lips. His eyes stare at me with a flicker of the wild fear he used to have in his eyes when there was a mamba in the grass. I cry into his mane. His wheezing breath tells me Lucky Strike is right. It is Tomtom's time. There is no dodging this black mamba of death.

When my father comes home he tells me to stay on the veranda. He walks down to Tomtom, his shotgun in hand.

I see him pat Tomtom's head and then stand to load the barrel. I feel Lucky Strike's hand on my shoulder. I see Tomtom's head jolt, just before the shot cracks in my ears. I cry, closing one hand on Grandpa Barter's knife in my pocket and clench the other so my nails dig into my palm.

– I am sorry, young baas, mumbles Lucky Strike.

My father walks back to me. I sense Lucky Strike drift into the shadows of the house. My father ruffles my hair.

– Hey Gecko, he says to me, life is hard. Sometimes you have to do things you'd rather not.

My father comes home with a stray tiger-lily cat to cheer me up after Tomtom is fed to the lions in the zoo. I call her Lalapanzi, Zulu for *lie down*. She dozes in the sun on the roof of the Chev, on the zinc roof of Beauty's rondavel, or on the firebox. Out of reach of Dingaan and Dingo.

She peels herself out of shadows to stalk the shifting sun. In the cool of dusk you may see her weave through hibiscus after fieldmice and rats. She loves to cart her catch into the house in her teeth, drop it and hunt it again out of dark corners. In the end, she coolly cages it in her claws and squeezes until the flicking tail gives up flicking. Then Lalapanzi scatters bones and fur for Beauty to pick up.

At night I hear a scratching coming from the bathroom because Lalapanzi uses the tub as a larder to store fresh victims. They run round and round as if they are about to be sucked down the plughole. My father lets Lalapanzi keep the rats. Fieldmice and moles he rescues from the tub with his bare hands. He pinches them behind the head and carries them down to the hibiscus jungle. Lalapanzi mews at his heels, her tail jerking with the unfairness of it.

My father is never scared. He picks up cold frogs and fuzzy, lizard-eating spiders and flicks them out the window as coolly as if they were jacaranda pods. It is only when he finds a black mamba in the garage that he sweeps it into an old gumboot, and shoots the boot full of birdshot.

# blood

My mother jogs Zane and me out of our beds. We follow her gas lamp out into the dark of the hoojoo owl, of the slithery mamba and the slinky rat. I pinch the hem of my mother's skirt. Out in the yard, we skip over the wire of the rabbit hutch. My mother tips up the Indian tea box. A white mother rabbit blinks red eyes at us. Zane and I gape gog-eyed as sopping, bald babies plop out of her into a lamplit world. For a moment they lie stunned in the mother's blood and juice, then they nose blindly after milk.

– Isn't birth beautiful? my mother purrs.

For me there is nothing beautiful in the bloody, pink, blind things. But I know I will love to hold them against my cheek when they get fur, so I nod. My mother smiles at me and I feel it is worth the lie.

Few of the babies will survive. A hawk will swoop down on them, or a mamba wiggle through the wire, or

– Sometimes the mother rabbit chews up her babies if she smells the human smell of your hands on them, whispers my mother.

It is cruel of the mother to kill her babies just because she smells us on them. I stare at her red eyes, at her wiggling, split-skin nose, and I want to hurt her.

⊜

The scratching comes to me from the bathroom. My heart drumming, I patter on bare feet through the dark. I flick the switch and the light-bulb floods yellow into the tub. Scared, button eyes look up at me out of a ball of pulsing rabbit fluff.

⊜

Frogs squeeze through the crack under the front door and go *plop plop plop* through the murky house. I lie dead still, thinking it may be the footfalls of the tokoloshe, the red-eyed, mischievous hobgoblin of the night, who uses the magic stone in his hand to witch himself into a smoky ghost, to seep through cracks. I hear the blood-fizzing yowl of a pig on the wind and the haunting *uhoo uhoo* of the 'hoojoo' owl. The gnarled old lemon tree outside our window taps against the pane as if it wants to flee the dark.

Zane sleeps like a dog through the farty plop of the frogs, through pig yowls and owl howls, through the tapping of the lemon tree. I run to his bed and pinch his dummy out of his mouth. My mother finds me like that at sunrise, when the nkankaan goes *ha ha haaa*. She never says a thing about a boy of seven with a dummy in his gob. Maybe she knows how scary everyday things like pigs and lemon trees can be at night.

My mother senses things, somehow.

⊜

I am with my mother in OK Bazaars. I see a rag doll with a flowery pink dress and yellow wool for hair. I stare at the beautiful doll but I know boys are not free to play with dolls. Boys kill birds and play with bows and arrows and cricket bats and rugby balls. Boys don't fiddle with flowery things. Not boys who want to be warriors or cowboys.

I glance at my mother. She drops a bag of Impala maize meal into the trolley for Beauty. She wipes her hand on her skirt, clouding the cloth.

I stare at the doll again, so beautiful. Without a word, my mother picks up the floppy doll and flips her into the trolley. My mother winks at me. My heart goes haywire as a monkey wedding, when rain falls out of a sunny sky.

⌐

Jamani yells and writhes in the grass. Beauty and my mother come running out of the house. Beauty wails as if Jamani is dead. My mother sees the telltale red dots of snake fangs in the yellow heel skin.

– Fetch a sharp knife, snaps my mother's firm, nurse voice.

I reach into my pocket for Grandpa Barter's Swiss Army, the knife that saved the Siamese princess.

My mother cuts Jamani's heel and sucks it. He cries blue murder. Beauty keens. Dingaan and Dingo bark. My mother spits venom and blood on the grass. Then she sucks Jamani's heel again. Suck, spit. Suck, spit. Till she is sure it is just blood in her mouth. Then revs up the Chev and drives flat out to the hospital in Howick, with Beauty and Jamani in the back.

When my mother comes home, she says the doctor said Jamani will survive.

– You saved his life, I tell her.

– I'm a nurse, she smiles.

At supper Lucky Strike tells Zane and me in the way he always does to make us feel that life is full of drama and adventure:

– Yo yo yo. Your mother is brave. If she was a man she would be a Zulu warrior.

O God of the assegai and the bones, let me become a warrior, brave in war, brave against lions or tigers. Not scared of snakes or sounds in the dark or the tokoloshe. Not a scaredy cat who runs away.

# hobgoblin

In the kindergarten run by nuns, I stare out of the windows in the direction of the farm. A ruler cracking down on my head jolts me back to the singing of *Jesus wants me for a sunbeam,* or *the farmer in the dell, the farmer in the dell, hey ho the derry-o, the farmer in the dell.* The nuns never tell us what a *dell* is or why we should sing *hey ho the derry-o* just because the farmer is in it.

Again and again the farm lures me away from the nuns and the singing. On the farm Jonas spikes snakes on a pitchfork and giggles spitty gums at our shrieks when he flings a dead but squirming snake at our feet. In the Zulu compound on the hill, bubbles gargle out of the nostrils of a sheep's head in a black three-legged pot. When chicken heads are axed, the headless chickens dart about the compound chased by Zane and Jamani and the other Zulu boys and me, their beady-eyed heads still shivering on the block. The chickens zigzag haphazardly, tricky as the bounce of a rugby ball.

In the Zulu huts: a smell of woodfire smoke, the taste of corn cobs on the flames, the feel of putu pap squeezed inside a fist. Newspapered walls and cheap, chipped china and grassmat floors and Soweto jazz on the radio. Beds propped high on bricks out of reach of the stumpy tokoloshe. My father laughs at the Zulu men for being scared of a short-ass, baboony thing. I just hope the to-koloshe is after Zulu boys rather than me and will go for Jamani in the backyard rondavel.

At the door of Lucky Strike's hut in the compound, his old, elephant-skin father sits on a stump, gazing runny, tobacco eyes across the deep kloof to the hills, where the past hides among dassies and monkeys. The past was when he stood at the gate of his kraal in the setting sun, counting the fat cows he would pay for a barrow-hipped wife. Counting cows in the days before the long foot-trek to Jo'burg and the white man's mines.

But Jo'burg is far away and I only know life at school and on the farm, where Zane and Jamani and I chase lizards and end up with a tail wriggling in our fingers as the lizard flees into a black crack. We pelt each other with clay down by the river. We fish the river for black bass and bluegill, with bamboo rods and earthworms on the hook. Sometimes we see a likkewaan in the river and fling stones at it, as if it is a crocodile.

⌒

My blind, batty great-grandmother, Grandmama Rudd, is to visit from the old home in Pietermaritzburg.

– Why do we have to fetch her? I whine in the Chev on the way to pick up Grandmama.

– The farm air is good for her, Gecko. Now, you be sweet to her, you hear? My mother frowns.

I just sulk and fiddle with the radio dials.

– One day I will be old and I hope you will come and fetch me to visit, she teases.

I dare not tell my mother that I sulk because of Grandmama's stale smell and the stink of her pee in the pot under her bed and her creepy, flaky-skinned hands, and her blind, smoky eyes. She scares the wits out of me, the way she blindly floats her long white hair and bloodred gown through the cool dark of our house.

Grandmama has a habit of ghosting out of the gloom, giving me a swift kick up the ass. Out of the way Box, she grunts. I skid across the pine floorboards that Beauty waxes on hands and knees. Box was the dog my mother and father gave me on my first birthday. They said I patted him, tugged his ears, rubbed his nose on my chin, then dropped him into my toy-box and closed the lid. So it was that my birthday dog came to be called Box.

One day Box ran away and though we called him for days he never came back. After Box went, my father came home with the black Labrador pups, Dingaan and Dingo.

Box is long gone, and I believe Grandmama knows that it is me and not Box in her way. Somehow she senses I hate her potty pee and flaky hands, so she foots me across the floorboards. I wish she was dead.

The only time I do not wish Grandmama dead is when she tells the story of the ice girl, and the story of Jake-up-a-tree. Grandmama married a man in England in the days before motorcars and aeroplanes and her smelling and blindness. They went out to Canada to find gold. There, in a shantytown, a girl died in winter. She fell through the ice while skating and they broke the ice downriver to fish her out. They could not bury her in the frozen earth, so she was kept in a box till spring. In the spring they lifted the lid of the box to discover that the girl's hair and fingernails had grown. When a Red Indian called Jake died in the same frontier town, they did not bother to make a box for him but put him in a sack and strung him up a tree until graves could be dug again.

– Tell me the story of Jake-up-a-tree, I beg her again and again.

Sometimes she tells me, but mostly she just drifts hobgoblinly through the dark.

⌒

When Grandmama dies in the old home in Pietermaritzburg I get to go to her burial. It is funny to see my father, the farmer, in a suit and tie, his hair Brylcreemed down, his Italian shoes gleaming.

– Like a real gentleman, my mother smiles.

She kisses him on the cheek. I feel so happy, I almost forget we are all fancy just to see Grandmama dead.

In the church Grandmama Rudd lies in a lidless coffin. My mother and father think I might dream about Grandmama if I see her dead, but I want to. Though I was scared to death of her alive, I feel no fear of her dead. Perhaps it is because I know she can no longer drift up darkly from behind.

Granny Rudd has railwayed all the way down from Zebediela in the far northern Transvaal to bury her mother. I am all wound up for she is to stay with us on the farm afterwards and will play dominoes and mikado with me.

– The old dear's in heaven, my mother whispers to Granny.

I stare long and hard at the wrinkled face and ghost hands of Grandmama. I feel no pity for her, just a longing to pinch her skin to see if it is as cold as frog skin.

Granny Rudd winks at me, as if to say: sweet boy. If she knew I had wished her mother dead she would not wink at me.

– Are you sad your mother's dead, Granny? I whisper, but it carries over all the sniffling and fidgeting.

Granny sobs and my father cuffs me on the head. I wish I could lasso the words, but they float out of reach, out there among the sweet incense and the fluttering candle flames and the Holy

Ghost. Like dragonfly wings. I am sent out in shame. Fool boy, the sour frowns of the grown-ups say.

Out to where Beauty is looking after Zane, who is kicking a yellow beach ball among the gravestones.

Sun-melon yellow. Sunflower yellow. An undead colour.

# cowboys and Indians

I am to go to school to get an *ijoocajun*, otherwise they will jail my mother and father. I stare out the rear window of the Chev at Zane and Jamani, standing at the gate and waving as if they will never see me again.

We wear khaki uniforms at the school in Howick. We line up in rows when the bell goes, so we look like dwarf Englishmen marching off to fight the Boers. Though there are no Afrikaans kids at the school in Howick, we still play war-war during play-time. None of us wants to be a Boer because they lost the war, but some unlucky English kids have to be Boers, just as you some-times have to be a Red Indian in cowboys and indians. It is the luck of the draw.

A smell of chalk dusts through Miss Fish's classroom. When the chalk breaks in her hands and scratches across the blackboard it makes my blood shiver. A pale, bony girl called Sarah sits in the back row with me. She hides her half-nibbled sandwiches under the flip-up lid of her desk. She begs me to let her sit on my hand. I let her. She follows me around at playtime and tries to kiss me until I stick my tongue out at her with a zebra silkworm wriggling on it and she runs away, crying.

Under Miss Fish you do not have the freedom to sit where you want to, or to pee during class, or to ask a question without your hand up in the air. Miss Fish keeps her pencils in a Royal Baking Powder tin. If you put your hand up to tell Miss Fish you have to go, she hands you the tin to pee in. So you just pinch until playtime or the end of the day. I am scared of Miss Fish, for her eyes change shape behind her glasses, like the bottled monkey foetuses and pickled snakes on the classroom shelf. Miss Fish does not believe in hiding the truth from us.

– Stand by your desks, she yells out of the blue.

We jump to our feet and stand at our desks with palms turned down to show Miss Fish that our hands are scrubbed. If she finds dirt under your fingernails, or if your fingernails are jagged from biting, she flips your hand over and stings it with her ruler.

– Only savages bite nails and hide bread under their desks, spits Miss Fish.

A horsefly sting. A bee sting. A bluebottle sting. Each sting stings sorer.

She checks under your desk lid for frogs and things. I sometimes get stung for smuggling a molesnake into class in a jam jar. Though everyone knows that molesnakes are harmless as earthworms, Miss Fish yells as if she just found a deadly mamba in my desk. Miss Fish wants all snakes dead and bottled.

Miss Fish teaches us about Jan van Riebeeck, the Dutchman who discovered the Cape. He is the founding father. Before Jan van Riebeeck came from Holland a few bare-ass Bushmen huddled in caves painting childish figures on the walls, lazy Hottentots lay in the sun while their cows grazed, and bloodthirsty Zulus and Xhosas wardanced around fires.

– If it wasn't for Van Riebeeck you would all still be running around naked like savages waving assegais and kieries, says Miss Fish, waving her ruler.

When she says things like that, I wish Jan van Riebeeck had not come along from Holland. Then we would run naked with assegais and kieries rather than sitting stiff in desks, writing down words words words from the blackboard. I wish a Zulu assegai would fly through the window and spear Miss Fish dead. Pin her to the blackboard.

Miss Fish teaches us about Blood River. The Zulus came over the hills in waves, but the Voortrekkers shot them down from behind their wagons. She always gets frothed up about the way the Ncome River turned red with Zulu blood.

In my mind I see a monkey foetus in a floating bottle in a river of blood. Its mouth gapes an O at me, but no sound comes out.

One boy called Si puts up his hand:

– But Miss, I thought blacks had black blood.

The class bursts out laughing. Even Miss Fish laughs at Si. I feel sorry for Si who does not know blacks bleed red just like us.

After school, I sell Si a molesnake for fifty cents. Dirt cheap.

– I'm going to be a missionary when I'm big, says Si, stroking the snake. And you?

If I was free to be anything, I would be a gardenboy like Jonas, or a cook like Lucky Strike. But these are no jobs for whites, that much I know. Miss Fish taught us that Indians are waiters and shopkeepers, coloureds are fruitpickers and fishermen. I fancy running a café and sucking niggerballs all day, spitting the balls into my hands to see the rainbow colours come out as my gob melts them down. But then you have to be Greek or Portuguese for that.

Being a farmer, like my father, is hard, for you have to do

blood things: brand cows with hot steel until the stink of singed hair fills the sky, clip chinks out of the ears of baby pigs, shoot stray dogs that chase the sheep. You have to hope the Zulu rain-makers make the rain fall and that the black locust clouds do not drift this far south.

Unless I could be a teacher of just one child, like Grandpa Barter was when he tutored the prince of Siam, I would never become a teacher. I hate the bloodshiver chalk across the blackboard and the dust you breathe in when you tap the dusters clean.

– Me, I'm going to be a cowboy, jus' like Clint Eastwood, I tell Si.

I balance Tomtom's saddle on my father's old Honda 125 in the garage. I am a rodeo cowboy in full swing, rocking and yahooing, lassoing the Chev's tailfins. Then the motorcycle topples over, scratching the Chev. I hope to God my father will not see the scar on his motorcar.

But he does, and he calls Jonas into the garage and blames him for scratching the Chev. Jonas stands with his hat in his hand, shaking his old grey head.

– Aikona master, aikona, Jonas says.

There are milky tears in his eyes. My father does not believe him. He calls Jonas a liar, tells him the money to fix it will come out of his pay. I watch Jonas shuffle away down the driveway.

Then I go up to my father, my heart in my mouth.

– It was me Dad, I mumble.

My father pinches my ear, bends me over the Chev, and beats me bare-handed on my ass until I howl bitter tears.

– Now you run and tell Jonas you're sorry. You hear me?

I nod and run after Jonas, clutching my ass.

He turns when he hears my feet thupping in the dust.

– Sawubona, young baas. I see you.

– I'm sorry Jonas, I sob.

Jonas puts his hand on my head.

– Not to worry, young baas. Jonas knows, he smiles tooth-lessly.

He dabs a handkerchief at his eyes and then shuffles on again, bent as the old lemon tree.

# cobras and crocodiles

Grandpa Rudd came out from Scotland to South Africa to seek his fortune in 1930. It was a poor, gloomy time overseas. One brother went to university in Edinburgh. The others had to find their own way in the world. Another brother went to New Zealand. He was captain of a boat that was sunk by the Germans during the war. My grandpa did not fight Hitler. He stayed up in Zebediela in the far north of South Africa and farmed oranges.

In his cravat and long khaki shorts, he smokes a pipe all day long, blowing cherry-scented smoke at the sky. He has read all the books by the wise men of the world. He is forever mumbling Latin to himself.

He tells me, his *wee warrior*, about wonderful things, things you never learn in school: that the Latin word for the hoopoe bird that goes *hoo hoo hoo* is *upapa epops*. (The lollipoppy sound goes around and around in my mouth: *upupa epops upapa epops upapa epops*.) He tells me: in India the he-lions hunt, not like the lazy lion of Africa who has his wives kill buck for him; that a marathon is 26 miles, the distance from Marathon to Athens; that clownfish can change their sex if the female in the school dies; that Charles Lindbergh in 1927 was the first man to fly alone across the Atlantic; that Roger Bannister in 1954 was the first man to run a mile under 4 minutes; that there is a man called Mandela in jail on an island.

– The man who reads needs no teachers, my wee warrior, he tells me.

Granny Rudd was born in Durban and her father shot himself in the head when she was a girl. In her young days in Durban, when she was still beautiful, she used to play tennis on sand courts and go to balls. Men would book a dance with her by writing their names on her fan. Those days are gone. Still, every time she sees a jacaranda flower fall in the breeze it reminds her of the fancy ball gowns.

In the tangled yard of Granny and Grandpa Rudd's house in Zebediela, a butcherbird spikes frogs and lizards on thorns to dry out in the sun, a pomegranate drops ripe, split fruit in the dust. Black ants crawl into the bleeding, jammy red juice. There is a crazy cock that pecks hens and little kids like us. If you outrun the cock and reach the barbed wire, you can climb into Africa. Over the fence Old Hopalong, a pegleg hermit, keeps a zoo: puffadders in glass tanks flicker forked flames of blood as they melt mice in their looping, pipey guts. Lizard-eating spiders. Nile crocodiles.

The story goes that one of his crocodiles bit Old Hopalong's foot off. If he catches you, he will feed you to his crocodiles and it's bye-bye blackbird.

Zane and I are always on edge there, caught between the eye-pecking cock and Old Hopalong. The crocodiles look dead lazy in the sun, but dart like spit if they want you. If you escape their razor teeth, they whip you with their tails. The crocodiles hiss at the frenzy of the chickens Old Hopalong flings in. Then, with a long, gassy sigh, they glide into the moss-green water. They surface to snap a jawful of squawking feathers, then sink again to shake the life out of them. You may still hear a warped *kwaak kwaak* from under the water before the chicken dies.

Grandpa Rudd tells us that in winter the crocodiles slow their heart-beat down to two beats a minute. Something no human beings, other than a few Indian holy men in caves, can do. I wonder if Nelson Mandela has slowed his heart-beat down to survive jail.

In winter the crocodiles hardly flinch if Old Hopalong jabs his peg at them. They hiss and half-heartedly clack their teeth at the sky.

My other grandpa, Grandpa Barter, is from the Forest of Dean in England. He studied at Bristol and Oxford. I don't think he had to study hard – he just *read* English. After Oxford, he went out to Siam to teach Prince Vadoowasevi.

Granny Barter, from the same Forest village in England, sailed out to Siam to marry Grandpa when he wrote to her. She says Grandpa's writing was so romantic, she had no choice.

– You see how wonderful words are, Gecko my boy, Grandpa Barter tells me. Spin a few magic words and you fetch a wife to Siam, spin again and you are in Marrakesh, sipping ice-cold orange juice while cobras sway to the pipes of the snakecharmer, and voodoomen cast a spell on you.

Upon her arrival in Siam, Granny Barter climbed into a tall clay jar of water to cool down. Once in the jar, she could not wiggle out, so she cried for help. Siamese boys came running and gaped eavesdropping eyes through the gap under the roof.

Another time in Bangkok, Granny uncovered two cobras entwined in her linen drawer. Grandpa shot them through their hooded heads, and you can still see the scattered holes in the bottom drawer of Granny's wardrobe. My father says it is just woodworm, not birdshot.

Granny and Grandpa Barter play bridge with my mother and father on the veranda while the crickets go *cheep cheep* and Dingaan and Dingo snore. Zane is asleep, but I have come out again. I get away with it because Grandpa tells my father not to be so hard on me.

– Did I ever tell you I shot two cobras hiding in your Grandmother's linen drawer?

– You told me a hundred times, Grandpa. Tell me another story.

– Hmmm. Let me see. That time I shot the cobras, the duck-boat man was rowing by on the klong. That's what they call a canal in Bangkok, a klong. Well, he moored his boat when he heard the shots. When he saw me carry the snakes out onto the veranda, dangling from the barrel of my shotgun …

– You never touched them. You made the boy pick them up.

– Don't listen to your grandmother. She has the memory of a sieve. Well, where was I?

– The duckboat man, I remind him.

– Yes. The duckboat man came along the klong. Along the klong. Ha ha. Rhymes. Along the klong. He begged for the cobras because snake blood gives you good eyes.

My father shakes his head at this juju talk.

– And if a man eats snake he can make the girls happy, winks Grandpa.

– Bart, chides Granny.

She calls him Bart when he is in a mischievous mood.

– How can snake make the girls happy? I beg Grandpa to tell me.

– Bart, snaps Granny.

– Just Siamese girls or all girls? I nag.

– I will tell you when the cows come home, Grandpa smiles. There are things in the world you've not yet dreamed of.

Things overseas? I wonder, hoping he will drop a clue, the way he drops cigar ash on his lap. Granny is forever darning his cords where the ash burns through.

– Two spades, Grandpa bids, ignoring my begging eyes.

– Three hearts, calls my mother.

– I wish I had eaten the cobras, then I would not have to bother with specs, mutters Grandpa.

– Bart, Granny tuts. The stories you tell the children.

– No bid, calls my father.

– Four spades, goes Granny.

This calling of spades and hearts is mumbo jumbo to me. I wish grown-ups would not riddle the truth away from me till the cows come home. I want to know where Lucky Strike goes with the Zulu girls. I want to know why Zulu men pay cows for girls and why snake makes the Siamese girls happy. I want to know what undreamed of things are out there in the world.

Grandpa tilts another tot of rum into his Coca-Cola.

Granny and Grandpa Barter stayed in the land of cobras and crocodiles and Siamese dancers and white elephants until the War, when the Japanese came along with their bayonets and bamboo cages. Then they went to Egypt and Grandpa taught English in Cairo. He once ran over an Egyptian's foot in his black Morris only to discover that the Egyptian, like Old Hopalong, had a peg leg.

That was the kind of luck he had.

Then they had to move on again, because of the Italians fleeing Abyssinia. It is thanks to the Japanese and the Italians that my mother was born in Durban, South Africa, and that I was born in Pinetown, a banana boy.

In the mornings, Zane and I run to the guest room and jump on their bed. Granny laughs with glee.

– O God, O God, Grandpa grunts, fishing for his teeth in a glass.

Pink fish under a lemon sun.

Lemon squeezed on bass. Lemon to draw the sweet out of Coca-Cola. Lemon and Peel's honey to cure a cold. A slice of lemon to freshen up floating teeth.

– Language dear, Granny tuts.

– Tell us about Siam, Granny, Zane and I chorus.

And she tells us about a rockery that came alive with snakes at twilight and about a toothless sacred crocodile that crawled under the seats of a crumbling cinema in Bangkok.

Or she invents African stories for Mole and Toad and Rat. How Mole finds a mamba down his hole and is rescued by a mongoose. How Toad outwits a likkewaan by lying still as a stone. How Rat sails downriver in a milk can to see the sea.

– And what did Rat see? goes Granny.

– A rainbow of dolphins, a string of seahorses and a flock of flying fish, Zane and I chant.

– A school of flying fish. A flock of flamingos, a flock of tickbirds, a flock of any bloody thing that flies other than fish, Grandpa mutters.

A flock of aeroplanes, a flock of kites, I want to say, but don't dare.

Grandpa is in a better mood after his rhubarb, Jungle Oats and *The Natal Mercury*. He tells me about his Oxford days, 1934 to 1936: punting on the Thames, playing hockey for England, jumping from Magdalen bridge into a cold river after a night of wine and girls at the May ball.

Granny's tongue makes sucking sounds, like starving swift chicks. But that just spurs him on. He tells me that not only did he jump, but he jumped in with his dinner jacket on, and not only did he jump in with his dinner jacket on, but he did a somersault from the bridge. Some of the young men came out of the river bleeding, their bare feet cut by the cracked bottles on the river-bed.

– But not your Grandpa. I climbed up and jumped again. One Scot jumped in with his kilt and you saw it's true that Scotsmen wear naught under their kilt.

– Bart, pleads Gran. He's just a boy.

– Even girls got cock-eyed, Grandpa goes on. They jumped off in their ball gowns. Or with just their frillies on, he winks at me.

– Bart. You always go too far.

# monkeyman

There is a beating at the door late at night. I go into the hallway to find my mother at the door and two black men outside. Dingaan and Dingo, instead of going bezerk at the sight of black men at the door, just sniff at their heels. It makes me wonder if they are men who can weave magic. Sangomas, or maskandi, the travelling musicmakers. When they take off their hats, I recognise them as the two men who skinned an ox my father shot. Maybe the dogs snuff after a whisper of blood.

– Please Madam, where is the baas?

– He's out.

My father is away, fishing in South West Africa. They twist their hats in their hands, their eye whites wide with fear. I pinch the hem of my mother's skirt.

– Madam, the police are in the compound. We have no pass-book because we come from Mozambique. But the baas gave us a job.

The cowskinner who mouths the words casts his gaze at me.

– The young baas knows us. He knows we are good workers.

I nod to my mother.

– Why are you in this country? demands my mother.

I feel ashamed that her voice is so hard. The men look at me.

My heart beats in the shelter of my mother's skirt.

– We must feed our children, Madam.

My mother bids them follow her. The men don their hats again. The man who begged my mother bows his head at me and touches his palms together.

My mother hides them on the veranda, behind the stone columns.

The police come and this time the dogs go wild, until my mother yells at them. The police have a black man in the back of the van, his fingers through the wire, like a caged monkey.

– Sorry to disturb, Madam, but we were told two men ran into your garden. You seen no one? one policeman says.

– No one, says my mother.

I have never heard her lie through her teeth before.

– May we make a search, Madam?

– If you must, my mother nods.

Through the kitchen window I see the police shine a torch into Beauty's face on the step of her rondavel. She shakes her head. They go into the hut and come out again with Jamani kicking and wild-eyed, as if they will eat him. Beauty howls: *aaaaaaaaiiiii*. They let him go and he rabbits back into the black mouth of the hut.

Then they walk around the house. As they go past the veranda, the two men from Mozambique shift around the columns. I can see their scared eyes, and they can see me. The policemen shine their torches onto the veranda and my face is caught in a beam. The policeman waves at me and I freeze, praying my eyes will not glance sideways at the hiding men. Just a flicker of my eyes and they will be caged with the monkeyman.

In the end the policemen give up and drive away. White eyes and monkey fingers in the back. My mother lets the men inside and makes tea for them in the kitchen. Tea bags bleed clouds of red rooibos tea into white china, the china she saves for guests. Beauty and Lucky Strike and Jonas have enamel mugs and plates they keep under the sink. This is something I have never seen. Black and white sipping out of the same cups.

The men laugh with my mother at having tricked the police.

– Yo yo, Madam, we will have a story to tell our children at Christmas.

I long to tell Zane, who has slept through it all as he does through thunderstorms. But after the men have gone, my mother warns:

– You must not tell Zane or anyone, otherwise the police will come again and take me away in the back of the van. Cross your heart and hope to die.

– Hope to die, I swear.

# bundu

The jungly, tangly bundu Zane and Jamani and I spend our days exploring is no Oxford. Once we go beyond the fence, caracals or jackals may slink out of the tall grass. A boomslang may drop out of a tree and fang us dead.

I have an assegai, a javelin from my father's Pretoria school days. Zane and Jamani have catties. Jamani is so skilled with a cattie he can pot weavers off the telegraph wires. But my father gets cross if Zane or I kill weavers.

– You don't find something beautiful in the world often enough to kill it, he says.

Starlings we may kill. That is another thing.

My mother, being a woman, does not see that killing pesky starlings is not the same as killing weavers. My father laughs at her, and we boys do too. My mother is funny that way. She believes flowers have feelings, and ears. Sometimes she sings to them, or leaves the radio on for them when she is out. She forbids Zane and me to hammer nails into the old jacaranda, as if it might bleed.

Zane and Jamani and I discover the skeleton of a dog down a dry well in the forest. Patches of hair still cling to the bones.

When we tell Jonas, he says:

– That dog was the box dog of the young baas.

I wonder if the dead skeleton down the shaft, the shadow of the Box I loved, heard me calling his name when I searched far and wide. Maybe his yelps fell just short of my dull, human ears.

Beyond the well, deeper in the forest, Zane and Jamani and I find an abandoned motorcar, stripped of wheels and seats and doors. Lizards and scorpions skitter through its rust husk. The windshield is cracked, but still in place. We stone the glass and it fans into cobwebbed veins before caving in. Then we stone the headlamps. A motorcar that once whizzed along the open road, heading somewhere, is now an eyeless, dented shell, abandoned in the bundu.

I imagine James Dean's head flying through the windshield of his Spyder. While Zane and Jamani pick up broken glass, play-play diamonds, my yellow daydream-haze fades. I see bits of glass as bits of glass. The javelin is just a javelin, no assegai.

# hero

Zane and I find a steel box buried in Tomtom's paddock. We dig it up, hoping it is treasure. There is a rusty padlock on it, so Jonas crowbars it open. Inside the box are guns and bullets. My father calls the police, who come in a van with an empty cage.

One policeman tells us the ANC hid the box.

– The ANC?

– The evil men. They want to kill us all, the policeman tells us. You boys done something heroic for your country.

– Maybe you boys even saved some lives, the other one says.

⌒

Zane and I tell all the kids down at the polo club while my folks play tennis and we play polo on bicycles. I enjoy the awed look the polo kids give us, but I feel confused by the other time the police came.

I don't feel like a hero. I am not sure which side I am on. In the few films I've seen at the drive-in, or the cinema in Howick, I always hoped the one on the run from the police would get away. I thought that this must be something evil in me. Until my mother helped the men from Mozambique.

# trek

First, man lands on the moon to change the world. Now we are to move to the Cape. For me the Cape is as far away as the moon, or America.

We drive out the gates with Dingaan and Dingo and Amos behind us in the caravan and Lalapanzi clawing at my feet and Beauty and Jamani and Lucky Strike and Jonas waving in the driveway. I am sad, as I may never see them again. But there is the adventure ahead, and I do not cry for long.

I imagine the Cape as full of colour. For one thing there will be sweet oranges you can just reach out and pluck and, for another, there will be the Cape coloureds. I have never seen a coloured in Natal. I imagine they are black like the Zulus, but wear colourful clothes all the time, like the Durban rickshawmen, or the clowns in the Boswell Wilkie circus.

⁘

The house in the Cape is a thatched Dutch house in the valley where Bushmen once danced under the moon. In the valley, I discover, the coloureds do not always wear rainbow colours and the farmers do not grow oranges.

The Simonsberg, a stone dragon, gazes down on the insect folk in the valley below. The Berg River flows through the valley and onwards through the vineyards of Paarl and the yellow wheat fields beyond to the fishing town of Saldanha on the cold Atlantic.

The old Dutch houses in the valley glimmer tusk-white under the African sun. Behind the clay walls woodworms gnaw at yellow-wood beams. Malay and Hottentot slaves clayed, whitewashed and thatched these houses. The slaves harvested the grapes and danced barefoot in wine barrels to squeeze the juice out.

Today there are no slaves but the coloureds bend under baskets of grapes, under the glare of the sun. Slave bells still toll when a veld fire blazes and the coloureds are called to beat a firebreak.

The Bushmen are long gone. Just one nomad survives. A flapping scarecrow of a man, he walks all day long in his tatty rags from farm to farm, driving a Firestone tyre with two criss-crossed poles. He tows a box behind him. The box is tied to his hips with a fraying rope. Around his neck hang the keys he has picked up over the years.

The folk of the valley call him the Firestone prophet, for he mutters rumours of blood as he walks the valley from Paarl to Groot Drakenstein to Franschhoek. It is hard to tell if the prophet is coloured, or white gone dark under the sun. Maybe the day will come when no one bothers if he is one or the other, my mother says. Folk drop stale bread and bruised fruit into his box. He abandons his dark mutterings to tip his hat. Then he heels after his Firestone tyre again. His voice mingles with the clink of lost keys blinking like fish scales in the sun.

He walks under azure skies. He walks when snow lies on the Franschhoek mountains. He walks all day, until the sun goes down, blood orange, behind the Simonsberg.

# cobra head

The school bus rumbles and rocks over the Helshoogte from Stellenbosch, to pick up us white farmkids bound for the government school for boys in Paarl.

Through the windows: coloured kids walk in the dust to the local coloured schools, carting their books in OK Bazaars bags.

Zane and I huddle together at the front of the bus, dazed by the raw bulk of the rowdy, pip-spitting matric boys who sit in the back row. They have just one year to go in blazers, then they go to the border to kill Cubans. They leer at me whenever I glance at them. Here in the Cape, war-war is no longer a game.

The third day on the bus: a canna seed, catapulted from the back, stings my cheek. I spin around and the manboy in the middle of the back row beckons to me. His name is Spook.

My knees jelly as I stand. Through swimming eyes Zane looks up at me, big brother of nine. The gabbling around me ebbs away, and all eyes zoom in on me. The bald head of the driver is fixed on the road.

I drag my heels to the back. Two rows from the end, the bus lurches around a corner and I lose my footing. My hand lands on a bulging, woolly breast as I fall.

– Sorry. I-yai-yai-yai I fell, I stammer.

She, cheeks flaming, gawks down at her bare knees.

I surface through a wave of catcalls and whistling.

As I face Spook again, he is all teeth.

– So, you laaik girls' titties hey? grins Spook in the slow, syrupy voice of a policeman, or a postmaster.

The matric boys on either side of him bray with laughter.

– Answer me boy, or I'll bugger you up, says Spook through his teeth.

Spook's rock fist rears up like a cobra's head. I breathe in the stink of his sweat. There is no doubt in my mind that he would beat me up at the drop of a hat.

I search his blue eyes for a hint of pity. There is none.

– I'm sorry. I didn't mean to. I just fell and —

– Stan' stiff when you talk to me, Spook barks.

I stand stiff as a broom.

– Juz your third day on the bus, an' you already fresh with the girls, hey?

In the corner of my eye I make out the wriggling of the poor girl.

– We can't have this sort of thing happening in a Christian country.

The big boys snigger at his wit.

– Now all you have to do is turn around, and tell her you sorry you touched her titty.

I have never felt so abandoned, and tears squirt from my eyes. I gaze down at my feet to hide my tears. This is no comfort, for my shoes have a pumpkin-orange tinge to them. My mother bought me orangy shoes instead of the uniform brown all the other boys wear. I am ashamed of my stand-out shoes and the nickname Pumpkinshoes Miss Hunter has given me.

– Go on, before I give you good reason to cry.

I turn to face the blushing girl.

– I'm sorry I touched your titty, I mutter, wishing I would die.

– Forget it, mouths the girl.

But I will never forget it.

# blue murder

Miss Hunter loves to hit boys on the hand with her wooden ruler. Afterwards, you rub spit on your hands to cool them down.

Now Miss Hunter is up on a chair, yelling blue murder and waving her ruler, just because of a white mouse. The mouse is my mouse, Oliver Twist. He was meant to lie still inside my shirt pocket, but he got too curious and peeked out.

– Put the bloody mouse in a box, yells Miss Hunter.

I tip Oliver Twist into a square chalk box and shut the lid.

Then Miss Hunter swoops down on me. She nabs me by the ear and frogmarches me to the boys' toilet. I think she is going to pull down my pants and beat me with her wooden ruler. Instead, she tells me to tip him in.

– Empty the box, boy.

– Please, Mevrou, don't drown my mouse, I beg.

– Your mouse is dead, Pumpkinshoes. Don't you be a hero now.

Plop, goes Oliver Twist, under the blue-tinted water. After a time, he bobs up, doggypaddling.

– Bloody vermin, Miss Hunter swears.

She yanks the dangling chain and he is sucked down the gurgling throat of the toilet. Just when I think Oliver Twist is gone forever, he bobs up again, his eyes black canna seeds popping out of his head with fear.

Again Miss Hunter yanks the chain. This time she jabs at Oliver Twist with her ruler, as a farmer dips sheep. This time he stays down.

⁂

Though I will never forget Miss Hunter sheepdipped Oliver Twist dead, she teaches us some good things about dying:

The Egyptians fish your brains out through your nostrils and bury you alive with your slaves.

The Romans put a penny in your mouth for the ferry to the underworld.

The Kalahari Bushmen bury you in a hole, with your bow and a quiver of arrows to hunt buck in the world of the spirits.

⁂

One time, when Miss Hunter is called to the office, a boy called Spud unzips his pink songololo in front of the class. Spud's head is full of potato and he is always up to no good. He still has his songololo out when Miss Hunter comes in. Her eyes flare and she jabs at his songololo with her wooden ruler. Spud hops from foot to foot. The hot-potato hopping is so funny we howl with laughter.

Then Miss Hunter holds his hand, palm up, and stings it over and over. Spud howls for mercy. Then she drags him out of the class by his sideburns. We stare out the window, empty our pencil boxes, flick through maths homework, anything to avoid each other's eyes.

Spud never comes to the school again. I hear he was caught pinching Camels from the Cape-to-Rio Café.

In South Africa, if the police catch you redhanded, and you are under 18, they tie you down and beat you, just for pinching cigarettes. The magistrate says how many cuts you get and there is nothing your father can do to save you, even if he is big in the fruit-canning business.

– You see what comes of fiddling, Miss Hunter tells us, after Spud is caught by the police. First you fiddle, then you swipe cigarettes, then you smoke dagga, and then you rob the Boland Bank or join the ANC. It's downhill all the way.

Lucky Strike smoked dagga, but he never swiped so much as a teaspoon from us. I wonder if Lucky Strike has run to Mozambique or Angola to join the ANC. Maybe he has traded his whittling knife for a gun. Maybe they have caught him by now and he is jailed with Mandela on Robben Island.

– Mandela and his Cuban friends in Angola want to hijack this beautiful country, Miss Hunter tells us. The godless Russians give them the tanks and aeroplanes. If it wasn't for our boys on the border, the evil men would burn this school, rape your mother and your sisters.

She lets this foot-fiddling thought sink in for a moment, then goes on:

– Now that Rhodesia is going to the dogs, South Africa is the last white, Christian outpost.

That is why, when we go to high school, we will march on Fridays. That is why, when we leave school, we will go to the army. We will fight to keep our mothers unraped, our schools unburnt, to stay on the God-given land. Though Mandela is behind bars, the Cubans are still out there, lurking in the Angolan bush, planning the big hijack.

Miss Hunter flops to the floor while chalking the blackboard full. Kobus de Jong runs for the headmaster, Meneer Theron. Meneer Theron huffs in, steering poor Kobus ahead of him, sure that this is a schoolboy joke. But it is no joke. Miss Hunter lies there, stone dead, black hairs jutting through her stockings and her eyes wide, just like the time Spud had his songololo out. Meneer Theron shuts her eyelids. I wonder if he will put a coin in her mouth for the penny ferry, but he just covers her up with the dusty tablecloth.

Then he shoos us out of the classroom, into the schoolyard. While waiting for the ambulance to come across town from Paarl hospital, he gives us each a hiding for driving poor Miss Hunter to the end of her wits.

Though Meneer Theron blames us for Miss Hunter's death, we are all made to go to her burial in school blazers, and look sad and sing sad songs for her. I am sorry we do not get a last gawp at her, the way it was with Grandmama Rudd. I wonder if they left her brain in. When the dominee goes on about how she is now in heaven with Jesus, surrounded by little children just like us, I wonder how Miss Hunter will get on without her wooden ruler. The dominee smiles at us, reminds us that Jesus said suffer the children to come unto me. Meneer Theron glares at us, as if to say: I'll see you hang from the yardarm.

I wonder if Jesus' heaven and the Roman underworld and the Bushman world of the spirits are the same place, or if every colour has a heaven, just as every colour has its own school. My mother told me: All loved things have a spirit, and go to heaven. I loved

Box and Oliver Twist, so they would have floated up from their wells and drainpipes. Granny Rudd loved Grandmama, so she will be footing some poor dead boy up the ass. And, as it turns out, Miss Hunter was loved, for her son drove all the way down from Messina in the far north for her burial.

After the burial my mother cooks I&J fish fingers and chips to cheer me up, and my father lets me sip the foam off his beer. It's a magic moment.

# dog days

All summer, Ford tractors with fruit-laden trailers clang down the bluegum avenue. The fire-sun saps all green, the dams dry out and the clay cracks into tortoise-shell patterns. Frogs creep under the clay shell into the hot damp ooze below and wait for the rains to fall again in June. Cow-tails swish flies from dung-flecked hides. Fly-stung fruit drops into the sand to rot. The stinging sound of cicadas is like a pine needle needling your eardrum.

Zane and I eat peaches and pears and grapes until we get gyppo guts. We play cricket on the front lawn with spindly Kala and sulky Langtand, who live in the nearby coloured town of Pniel, on the road to Stellenbosch.

Flip van Staden, whose father is poor and works at the sawmill on the railway, is shy and just hangs around on the fringes. Flip is freckled and white, like Nesquik sprinkled on vanilla ice-cream.

Sometimes Bach, the German boy who lives down the road, drops by and bowls a few balls.

The tall pines around the lawn are part of the game. If you hit a ball at a pine without a bounce, you are out, as if caught. There is also the risk of the dogs catching the ball in their teeth and running into the vineyards with it. So many balls are buried in the vineyards that I imagine revisiting the valley one day as an old man to find an orchard bearing cricket balls as fruit.

Our thatched house at the foot of the Simonsberg is cooled by wide whitewashed walls and shaded by tall pines and an old bluegum. The bluegum is bent by a climbing bougainvillaea, a fountain of pink. My father always says it is the highest bougainvillaea in Africa.

– Open another bottle of Roodeberg, my father jokes, the bluegum may come down tonight and kill us in our beds.

– In for a penny, in for a pound, nods Grandpa Barter, holding out his glass for a refill of red.

Since Granny and Grandpa Barter followed us down to the Cape from Natal, they come over at dusk for sundowners on the veranda. In front of the veranda a shaggy-bearded palm sways in the wind.

Within the walls it is dark and cool. It smells of the Dubbin wax Mila, the Xhosa gardenboy, rubs into my father's boots, and the Malayan bobotie that Nana, our coloured maid, cooks. And, at night, it smells of wet dog, for my father runs the dogs up to the dam on the back of his Isuzu 4x4 bakkie for a swim at dusk.

Under the grass in the front yard is a brick cellar. To Zane and me it is a hideout. A bomb shelter. We stock it with Oros Orange and Ouma rusks and kudu biltong. You never know when the Russians will come, or when the bluegum will come down on the folks and orphan us.

You can climb the gnarled lemon tree up onto the zinc roof of the garage and lie there, among the ripening pumpkins and the smell of pines on the breeze and wafts of cow dung ploughed into the vineyards. If you close your eyes, the sigh of the pines filters through the clank of tractors, the cry of guineafowl and the barking of dogs, and the sun swirls colours behind your lids.

We head over the Simonsberg to Bikini Beach. Zane and me and the paddleski and picnic basket and icebox and deck chair and dogs bundled on the back of the Isuzu 4x4 bakkie. The dogs bark whenever they see another dog, till their gobs froth and fling strings of drool to the wind.

We go through the Strand, along the seashore, to Bikini Beach, tucked away behind Gordon's Bay harbour. My father sinks into his deck chair to read *The Sunday Times*. He frees his toes from his farm boots and wiggles them under the sand. There is no way he is going into the water when he can stay in his deck chair with the *Sunday Times* bikini girl.

I wait for a big wave to gather and just as it is about to curl I run and dive from the sand. In mid-air I see a shark gliding through the curved wave. Time stops for a moment, a blink of the eye, the way it does when Wile E. Coyote runs off the edge of a cliff and his feet pedal the sky before he plummets to earth. I hope to God it might be a dolphin, but then I see the gills, four gouged commas after the full stop of his eye. I windmill my arms, as if to rewind my flight through the air.

The cold sea swallows me. I flap and pedal to the surface and the next wave dumps me on the sand. The shark is gone. I stare at my feet and hands, all the scot-free fingers and toes, and fill my lungs with air to cry.

# Vespa dreams

Saturday night: Granny Barter gives Zane and me Coca-Cola to drink while we gawk, gog-eyed, at the box. There is never Coca-Cola in our old, muttering, juddering Westinghouse fridge at home, unless Zane or I have a runny tummy, and then my mother gets a bottle from the Pniel Café and stirs the Coca-Cola dead flat to cure us.

– If you leave a jammed, rusty nut in Coca-Cola overnight, the Coca-Cola will eat the nut loose from the bolt, my father tells us.

Zane and I do not mind if Coca-Cola eats nuts and bolts, or rots teeth so we will end up with false teeth in our gobs like Grandpa. We love Coca-Cola and watch to see Granny pour to the same level for both of us. A litre of Coca-Cola fills four of Granny's glasses and a bit. Zane and I always fight over the left-over bit till Grandpa calmly tips it into his rum.

On their black-and-white TV I see James Dean dicing motor-cars in *Rebel Without a Cause* and Gregory Peck hunting Moby Dick. But the best film ever on the box is *Butch Cassidy and the Sundance Kid*. For days after, I ride through the orchards on my bicycle, singing *raindrops keep falling on my head*. The coloured fruitpickers shake their heads at the sight of a white boy singing raindrops in the flaming Cape summer.

While I ride my bicycle on the farm, or bounce a tennis ball against the garage wall, or lie on the garage roof, drifting to the sigh of the pines, I dream of being a film star like Paul Newman or Robert Redford. In my dreams I sip Japanese-umbrella cocktails in seaside cafés, somewhere in the wide jigsaw world, far away from Spook and Miss Hunter.

Now, as we sip Coca-Cola, Cliff Richard and his chinas zoom along in a London bus.

– I once went to a dance with Cliff Richard, chirps my mother out of the blue.

My mother has told me of her nursing days, riding a Vespa along the Durban seafront, skirt and hair up high, whistling at the surfers, dancing on the beach. Even now, in her thirties, she whirls her skirt like the fanned tail of a peacock when she does the twist. Still, the thought of my mother, who talks to her flowers, flirting with a film star is far out.

– Well, I didn't dance with Cliff, alone, but he was there, with his band, The Shadows.

I imagine The Shadows as black, flapping, shadowy moths.

– I wore a pretty red skirt with white polkadots and hoped I might catch his eye. After all, I had good legs, says my mother.

I see my mother with red lipstick, in a polkadot skirt, twirling red like a flame, scattering shadow moths to the wind. And Cliff Richard, swinging his hips close to her soapstone legs.

– You went out looking like a Point Road whore, grunts Grandpa.

– What's a whore, Grandpa?

He winks at me.

– I'll tell you one day, he says.

– It's a rude word and I never want to hear you say it, my father chips in.

– Then howcome Grandpa gets to say it?

– Because Grandpa's a zany old fool who drinks too much rum, says Granny.

I have never heard her call him a zany old fool before and imagine Grandpa will spit his teeth out in a splutter of fury. But Grandpa just winks at me again.

– So, did he ask you to dance? I nag my mother.

Surfacing from memories of fanning skirts and stovepipe jeans, she says:

– Who?

– Cliff Richard, Mom.

– No, he didn't dance with me, or any other girl. He just stared into the eyes of one of The Shadows all night.

I feel sorry for my mother as the moon chases our Peugeot 404 home along the Simondium road. If Cliff Richard had danced with her, things might have turned out otherwise. Zane and I would drink Coca-Cola instead of the Oros Orange you mix with water. We would have a colour TV and my mother would have a machine to wash the dishes.

Sometimes, while washing up over weekends when Nana is off, my mother tells me never to give up on my dreams. By the way she says it I know that some time ago, somewhere along the way, the dreams of the flirting, miniskirt girl on the Vespa fell to the wayside.

The moon dogs the 404 home. We go past the Simondium Hotel, where coloureds cluster outside the bottle store on Saturday mornings to stock up on weekend jerepigo after a week of picking fruit in the sun. Swaying men bend under jerrycans of sweet wine, like the refugees you see on the box, their world on their backs. Past Weltevreden, where Lars's father farms cows and pigs and where the moon paints abstract white patches on black-and-white cows.

Lars, my Danish neighbour over the road in Lofthouse. My hero, five years older than me. He is half fish and half footballer, shoulders wide from butterflying around the dam, his calves the size of pawpaws from footing the ball into the goal for the Paarl football club.

The 404 rattles across the railway line and past the sawmill, where Flip van Staden's father saws hills of sawdust. Poor, shy, freckled Flip. Nesquik scattered on vanilla ice-cream.

On we go, past Boschendal. The Cape Dutch gables ghost white against vineyards of black satin.

It was on this sawmill road, running past Boschendal, that I once saw a coloured boy stone a river crab as it scuttled and scratched across the tar. He flung the stone like a schoolboy spinning a top and I heard the crab crack.

As the 404 swings into the yard, the headlamps pick up Lalapanzi's eyes and Dingaan and Dingo jerk awake and bark and jig in the glare, daring to bite the spinning tyres of the Peugeot, leaping back just before being run over. You would think they too had seen *Rebel Without a Cause* on Granny and Grandpa's box.

# dodging death

The dogs dodge death: biting the Peugeot tyres, catching snakes and seeking fights with the neighbour dogs. Lalapanzi dodges death running across the grass. The Cape eagle owl in one of the stone pines swoops down at her and sometimes snatches a flutter of cat hair. During the day Lalapanzi dozes under deck chairs in the yard, under the vines, under the Peugeot, anywhere where there is a roof so no claws drop out of the sky. She used to follow the sun. Now, in a neverending game of hide-and-seek, she darts from one den to another.

Zane and I love to taunt Mila, until he drops his spade and chases us. We call him boy, although Mila is a man. With a family hundreds of miles away, in a mud hut in the Transkei, tending scrawny cows in the dongas and dust. Mila has an iron bed in the men's hostel on the farm. At Christmas he gets a holiday and a Christmas box from us: a shirt for him, sweets for his children and a head-cloth for his wife.

Sometimes we chat to Mila in a fanagalo mix of English, Afrikaans, Zulu and Xhosa. But most of the time he just watches us play cricket on the grass while he digs his hoe into the pine-shadow earth, where hibiscus and oleander spill colour.

– Oleander is beautiful but deadly if you chew it, my mother warns.

– Just the flowers? I wonder.

– The leaves too.

I tally up the ways to die in the Cape:

Be killed by a falling bluegum.

Be shot by the Russians when they come. (Russian Migs fly over Angola, just north of the border. In between there is just South West Africa. Just dunes and elephants and Hereros.)

Be poisoned by oleander.

My bicycle, a Chopper, is the reverse of a penny-farthing. The small front wheel is the cunning ploy of an inventor who wants boys dead. Whenever my eyes stray from the road and I hit a pot-hole the Chopper catapults me through the steerhorn handlebars.

– You'll be scarred for life, my mother cries as she dabs cotton wool and Fissan at my grazed palms and knees.

My mother has this thing about scars. She even had the school doctor give me my yellow fever shots under my feet, instead of on my arms. The other boys laughed to see me pull my socks off for the needle.

Zane and I cycle down the sawmill road to the Groot Drakenstein Games Club to watch my father play cricket. He bowls good spinners but is too reckless with the bat. He hits two or three balls over the boundary for four runs, then hooks a high ball that is caught on the boundary. He walks back to the pavilion, smiling, bat tucked under his arm the way the monkeys tuck corn cobs. Smiling because he would far rather be caught than bowled.

After my father is out, Zane and I play cricket too, behind the clubhouse, with Kala and Langtand and other coloured kids from roundabout. Or we play tennis on the sand court with threadbare balls and wood racquets. But the coloured kids watch from a wary distance when Zane and I dive into the pool for WHITES ONLY, though we all have mud between our bare toes, and hands sticky from the juice of stolen peaches.

My mother sends me on my bicycle to Pniel to buy a loaf of Springbok bread from the Pniel Café: a nook of a café jammed full of tins of Koffiehuis and Van Riebeeck coffee, boxes of Joko and Five Roses tea, Jungle Oats, tins of tuna, bars of Sunlight soap, Lion matches, combs, tartan-handled pocket knives, tomatoes, bananas and bolts of cloth.

Zane and I cycle through the vineyards and orchards to Weltevreden to frisbee dried cow dung at the cows, or to trap fat pigeons in the fodder bins. There, wobbly-footed calves suck your hand with sandpaper tongues until white drool drips from your fingers. Blind kittens litter the dark corners. Slimy piglets slide out of blood-specked sows. They lie still in the afterbirth in the sawdust, then fumble for milk. Through the stink of pig dung you get sweet wafts of udderhot milk and baled grass.

Zane and Bach and I saddle the stone wall of the bull kraal and gawk at his shotput balls and tapered horns. When the bull turns away, we leap down into the kraal to jab his backside with a stick. Then we claw up the wall again as he reels and snorts and pitchforks his horns at us.

One time I jump from the wall and dart in but slide on glossy dung, under the bull's hanging balls. The bull stamps me into the peanut butter of dung and mud a few times before a Xhosa man vaults the gate and tugs the bull off me by his ring.

Another way to die in the Cape.

If you are a black boy you hardly ever see your father. He is far away, on a farm in the Cape, or down a mine in Jo'burg, or in jail.

If you are coloured, you are bundled lock, stock and barrel on the back of a Bedford and dumped on the dusty, windy Cape Flats.

Me, I am a white boy in Africa. Every night my father tells me: Bona wena kosasa, See you tomorrow. And all tomorrows, at dusk, my father's dog-chased bakkie roars into the yard. He wades through the barking dogs and the stories Zane and I yap at his heels. Stories of pigeon-catching and bull-dodging.

So my tomorrows have always ended in that hair-ruffled feeling that the Russians will stay at bay and the bluegum will bend but never fall, that my father will never be jailed.

But tomorrow is another kind of tomorrow. It is my first day of high school. My uniform is laid out: grey shorts, blue shirt ironed by Nana. My Grasshopper shoes blink with the Kiwi wax Mila has rubbed in. Tomorrow is the first time I go to school with no juice bottle. High school boys do not drink out of juice bottles. My father has given me his fountain pen, and an inkwell of Indian Blue. High school boys do not write with pencils.

# Bulldog

The bus for whites, bound for the school for white boys in Paarl, hoots at the barefoot coloured kids who stray onto the road. They whistle and wave after us.

Flip van Staden and I, the two new boys, stand facing the big matric boys in the back seat of the bus. The matric boys are all seventeen or eighteen, giants to Flip and me. I hope not to cry as I did the time when Spook shamed me. High school boys do not cry.

A boy who goes by the name of Hotrod lays down the rules of the game. We have to echo his words. If we don't, he will make us suffer.

– Don't fool with me, warns Hotrod.

I stare at his hard, scarred fist. He has inked the word *Loverboy* along his knuckles. There is no way I want to fool with him.

– Say after me: My mother's a whore.

At the word *whore* there are hoots of laughter. Hotrod just sits there with a fat grin under his square Nazi-helmet haircut.

Grandpa Barter had said my mother went to the Cliff Richard dance looking like a Point Road whore, but my father had said it was a rude word.

I hear Flip stutter out the words:

– Ek kan nie.

– And you? Hotrod demands of me.

All eyes are on me. Though I would mouth the rude words with crossed fingers, to escape Hotrod's wrath, Flip's stand gives me no choice.

– I can't, I mumble.

I wish I could reel in the foolhardy words. All eyes switch to Hotrod.

– Then you two must kiss Bulldog, Hotrod barks.

The bus is a carnival of laughter as Bulldog is dragged to the back. She is wild-eyed and cursing.

– First you, rooinek.

I shut my eyes and lean forward to kiss her. Perhaps I shut my eyes because they always do in the Saturday night feature films on Granny and Grandpa's box. Perhaps because the sight of Bulldog before me is not something out of a romantic film.

I feel her lips against mine. Our heads are jammed together by hard hands. I am drowning in the baying laughter of the big boys. Her lips part and my teeth jolt against hers. The hands let go, and as my face flies from hers, she spits in my eye. I wipe her gob on my shirt sleeve.

After Flip kisses her and she spits at him too, Hotrod lets us go. In my seat I hide my head under my blazer and cry. Damn Flip, why did he have to be a hero?

This is my first kiss. It is sore and shameful. I can never undo it. Bulldog, eye-spitter, will always be the first girl I kissed. Serves me right for scaring poor, bony Sarah with the zebra silkworm on my tongue.

Paarl Boys' High: Flip and I join the other new boys herded onto the rugby field. We run through a tunnel of big boys who whip at our bare legs with their school ties. Then some boys are made to rub their balls against the rugby posts. Flip and I and others are given acorns. I imagine we will have to chew them. Instead, we go down on hands and knees and roll the acorns across the rugby field with our noses while the other schoolboys howl with laughter and the teachers drink tea in the staff room. Though the acorn rolling is slow and blind, the odd kick up the ass spurs me on.

# robbing God

On Sunday mornings my mother, Zane and I go to St George's church in the valley, while my father stays to read *The Sunday Times* in a deck chair, and light the vinestump braai for lunch.

Ahhh. My father's braais. The tang of burning vinestumps. The hiss and spit of fat. The whine of begging dogs. The smell of cooking meat, which is the smell God loves.

Inside the whitewashed church walls, the priest rubs his fingerless hand in his good hand, stained yellow by cigarettes.

I stare at his knobkierie stub while he conjures up a sandalled, bone-and-blood Jesus wandering through the sands of my imagination. I no longer see God as a raggedy, bone-rattling sangoma, but as the lonely, skinny man on the cross.

In St George's, this Church of England so far south of England, coloured and white gather under one roof. Still, the whites of St George's huddle together in the front pews, to drink the blood of Jesus from the cup before the coloureds do.

There is a doddering organist who turns our reedy singing into a burial song.

Out in the sun, a few miles up the road, my father is in his deck chair, one eye on the vinestump fire and the other on the *Sunday Times* bikini girl.

At the words *Draw near and drink the blood*, the organist abandons a hymn halfway through the last verse and hobbles down the aisle. Our voices drift on rudderlessly. The way she goes hobble hobble hop, hobble hobble hop, tells you that all her suffering for Jesus is forgotten in the sweet joy of being first to kneel at the altar rail, first to lift her lips to the blood.

The money plate comes round. A one-rand note flutters down from my fingertips. Then I dip my hand into the plate to finger out fifty cents change, to buy a Kit-Kat or Bar One at the Pniel Café afterwards. When I look up to see frowns, I sense I have done something taboo: fiddling out change from God's money.

When the priest tells us to *go in peace and serve the Lord* I run out and bury the fifty cents in the graveyard.

While we English pray to God in St George's church, the Afrikaans farmers of the valley gather at the Dutch Reformed church in Simondium, further down the road to Paarl. The deacons, in black and white, look like butcherbirds. A faint smell of mothballs and Kiwi shoeshine and Brylcreem is in the air. A domino ripple of nods follows the black-frocked dominee as he passes through his white flock.

In the old days, when farmers trekked from far afield in their oxwagons and Cape carts to reach church for the monthly nagmaal, the gathering of the clans would be a whole weekend affair. There would be outspanned oxen and tents and camp fires and men playing jukskei with ox-yoke pegs and women baking melktert and koeksisters.

But in the 1970s in South Africa there is little to break the quiet of the sabbath. There is no cinema. No shopping.

Sunday afternoon: Bach and I lie on the hot white pebbles on the banks of the Berg River and share our dreams. Bach wants to join the commandos and kill Cubans on the Angolan border. I want to be Robert Redford or Paul Newman and see the world at the end of the Atlantic where the Berg River runs to. Or, maybe, be Hemingway or Wilbur Smith and fish for wahoo in the Caribbean.

Bach's stomach is taut, and he has a patch of black ball-hair I am jealous of. He tells me about girls and sex, and that he once saw a coloured man's bare ass bobbing over a girl in the pines up by the dam.

– It's like the pigs on the farm, he laughs as he skims a pebble over the water.

I turn my face away from him to stare at the tiger's-eye river flowing by. Where it is deepest the water is almost black.

Two crocodiles have escaped from Safariland and found their way into the Berg River. It is in all the papers. Somewhere up or down river, they cruise through the murk and scum for the feet of lapping cows and yapping dogs.

Another way to die in the Cape.

Since I saw *Jaws* at the Protea Cinema in Paarl, I am scared of black shadows under the water.

My father told me a shark once jawed a boy a mile up the Tugela River. The shark should never have been there.

– That is irony, he said to me, being killed by a saltwater shark a mile upriver.

It is crazy to imagine a shark swimming a hundred miles up the Berg River from Saldanha Bay, just as it is crazy to imagine sharks lurking under my seat in the cinema. Still, I always tuck my feet up under me in the Protea.

The thing to do if a shark fins towards you, my father says, is to stay calm, not flap about like a wounded fish. If you see a mamba, act dead. If you see a lion, climb a tree. If an ostrich goes for you, jab a thorn branch at his eyes. And if you outfoot bulls and trick snakes and sharks, if you run fast and climb high, you may survive to see the world.

My dream of seeing the world beyond South Africa is like a honeybee that keeps homing in on your can of Coca-Cola and you get scared you might swallow it, for if it stings you, your windpipe clogs up and it's bye-bye blackbird.

This dream zithers in my ears and I cannot flick it away or shake it off. I hear the zither through the din on the bus and through the drone of teacher voices at school. And just as the honeybee finds the ringpull-hole in the can of Coca-Cola and suddenly drops inside and sounds dizzier, so this dream wriggles up a nostril and niggles inside my head.

# Stompie

Every Monday morning in Paarl Boys' High we file into the hall. The headmaster, Visoog Vorster, is feared for his run-up when he canes boys. While he tells us of God and other deep things, his fisheyes gander for a victim.

There is an unwritten law at Paarl Boys' High that you look Visoog Vorster in the eye while he is up there, an invading viking in the bow of a ship.

At Paarl Boys' High all laws are unwritten. You find out through hearsay, or by being caned for it, Lars told me.

While Visoog Vorster drones on, my eyes wander across the rows of grim teacher faces up on stage, to the honours boards bearing the names of Paarl Boys' old boys who have gone on to play rugby for South Africa. The names go hazy, drift out of focus.

I am up at the dam with Bach, making a raft out of wine barrels. We pitch a tent on the raft to camp out on the water. Above the tent flutters the tattered, moth-eaten Union Jack that long ago lay on the coffin of Grandpa Rudd's brother, killed in the war. During the night, water seeps into the barrels and into our sleeping bags. We abandon ship, and the Union Jack, having survived Hitler and moths and games of pioneers and Indians, sinks under the moon.

– You there, barks Visoog Vorster, jabbing his finger in my direction.

My heart jolts and I feel a sudden squirt of pee in my pants.

– You there, at the end of the third row, stand up.

Another new boy, scared white like me, stands up. Five hundred boys fix their eyes on the stumpy kid called Stompie. I'd rather run into Turkish gunfire at Gallipoli than change shoes with Stompie.

If Visoog Vorster is after your ass, Lars told me, you never get away with under three cuts. Three stinging cuts, drawn out because of the time Visoog needs for each run-up. Lars said he lets you choose from a row of bamboo canes on top of his cupboard before making you bend over his desk.

– What do you think you are doing, boy, looking around while I'm speaking?

Stompie sobs, but that just winds up Visoog Vorster.

– Wait outside my office and stop snivelling like a girl, he yells.

Stompie stumbles past frowning teachers, through a door under the photograph of the bald prime minister.

Having put Stompie in his place, Visoog Vorster calms down.

– You know, boys, Paarl Boys' did not become the foremost rugby school in the history of this land by giving in to feelings. Discipline is what has made South Africa strong. Boys from this school, boys who may have sat in the very chair you are sitting in now, have gone on to govern this land. Think of it.

Visoog Vorster glances at the prime minister.

– You know this isn't a country where things just fall into your hands like a ripe plum. You are not yet ready to understand politics. You have to leave that to us, who are older and wiser.

We nod, as if to say, yessir.

He goes on to read the results of the weekend rugby and a dozen teams stand up in turn. One boy, Franzi, scored a hat trick. He is cheered and called up to the stage to shake hands with Visoog Vorster himself.

The day I stand face to face with Visoog Vorster, I wonder if I will be a Stompie and be caned, or a Franzi and be cheered.

Hall ends with the singing of the school song and *Die Stem*. We stand stock-still, heads cocked at the orange, white and blue flag.

– We will live, we will die. Us for you, South Africa.

Back at our desks, we chant Latin. Stop. There is a *tok tok* at the door. It is no mischievous tok-tokkie who runs away *ha ha*. It is Stompie, sobbing and squeezing his ass.

The teacher bids him sit down. He gives Stompie a handkerchief, tells him to wipe his nose, not to be so melodramatic, that it won't kill him. Stompie flinches in his desk as if his ass is wired to a rat cage and the rats are gnawing the hell out of him.

A tap of the bamboo cane against the blackboard draws us back to our Latin.

– Amo amas amat amamus amatis amant, we chant in unison.

The bell goes and we stampede out.

As is the custom, Stompie jerks his pants down in the toilets. We gasp at the flaring red welts across his white ass. Stompie smiles. For us, Stompie, short-ass stub of a boy, is a hero.

# Cat Stevens

All day long it spins round and round in my head: my father is taking me to watch cricket at Newlands with him. I am over the moon. Zane, of course, is still too small, but I am thirteen and in high school.

As we drive out of the winelands and through the southern suburbs to Cape Town in my father's dusty Isuzu bakkie, the Beach Boys wish all the girls could be California girls. From the way they sing, I too wish they could all be California girls, though America is still as far away as it was when man landed on the moon. The Beach Boys catch the feelgood mood you feel when everything in the world is just dandy.

Newlands: my father and I sit on a crowded grandstand and look out onto the floodlit pitch, where Orange Free State in orange want to bowl out Western Province, being us, in blue.

My father, the cricket fundi, deciphers the game for me. When Zane and I play we make up the rules, so I'm not into the ins and outs of cricket, things like silly mid-on and gully and googly. Still, it's good to listen to him holding forth on a theme he loves.

Kirsten is batting and he sends the ball flying into the grandstand. All around us men yell *Prooooviiince* with such gusto that it ripples their bagpipe beer-guts.

– Want a Castle Lager? my father offers, casually.

I just blush and nod.

My first beer. Bitter, but I do not care a jot. My father winks at me, his son becoming a man, and I grin like a jackass.

On the far side, a carnival of coloureds begins a Mexican wave. The wave surges around the field, and as it reaches us my father and I jump up. Empty beer cans fill the sky, then rain down on unlucky heads. The wave goes round and round, till it dies out at the boxes, where the rich feel this jack-in-the-boxing is undignified.

A coloured vendor with no front teeth carts an icebox on his stomach.

– Howzabout a lolly to make you jolly, he calls, flashing pink gums.

– Coloureds pull out their front teeth because other coloureds find it sexy, whispers my father in my ear.

This lollyboy is the casanova of Cape Town, for sure, with his eltonjohn shades and gone teeth.

– Howzabout a sucker to keep you wakker, he jives.

Men chuck empty beer cans at him, playfully. He ducks like a boxer, just shifting his head.

My father forks out small change for a granadilla lolly for me.

Now I juggle a beer can in one hand and a dripping lolly in the other.

After my beer and granadilla lolly, I join the string of wheezing, bantering men wanting to pee. One, ahead of me, pinches his fly and rocks from foot to foot.

Further ahead there is a line of beer cans on the peeing wall, as the men are forced to put them down for a minute to unzip.

When I am tall enough to reach up and prop a beer can on the wall, I will also be a man.

Back in the grandstand I am just in time to see a man run bare-assed across the pitch with two policemen after him. With his shaggy black beard he reminds me of Cat Stevens on my father's record of *Tea for the Tillerman*. I feel a twinge of pity for him as he is as white and exposed under the floodlights as a rabbit in a motorcar's headlamps. He runs blindly and falls over the rail, then is up again, hopping through the whistling crowd. As the policemen hurdle the rail the crowd turns on them, booing.

I wonder if he will get away, or if the policemen will catch him and jail him with Nelson Mandela on Robben Island.

# dead fish

The afternoon bus rattles along dirt roads.

Past fields where convicts look up from their hoeing to watch us go by.

Past barefoot coloured schoolkids walking the long torrid miles in clusters of lurid colour.

I sit with my knees up against the seat in front of me and my blazer draped over my head for shade. The bus rumbles on, and I focus on its rhythm and the vibration in my feet.

We stop. I lift the corner of my blazer to look out.

There is a rundown café, with a solitary petrol pump in front and a faded rooibos tea advert on the zinc roof, where you buy the newspaper and Simba chips, or Springbok bread and fresh milk.

Bicycles are propped against the finger-dirt wall below a window jammed with Koffiehuis tins and Koo jams and Silver Cloud flour and batcollar pink shirts that were in fashion in the sixties, maybe. A small coloured boy sits in the doorway. A cockroach crawls across his dirt-caked toes. The boy catches it and tugs its legs off, calmly, one by one.

At home the summer smell of mown kikuyu grass beckons me. I dump my schoolbooks, shed my school blues and greys, my fears of bamboo and big boys, and run out the yard and up the bluegum avenue. Overhead, blades of light spear through the bluegums. A red and green pheasant darts across my path, giving me a scare.

A tractor rattles by, fruitpickers standing in the empty fruit bins, as if they are to be canned and shipped overseas. They wave at me and yell: baleka, baleka. Run, run. And I run, out of the bluegum avenue, past the reservoir, and on through pear and peach orchards, through the stinging cicada sun, up to the dam on the slopes of the Simonsberg.

I kick off my Dunlop tackies and denim shorts and dive in, plummet down through the lukewarm surface layer into the icy depths, feel the usual sharp panic that I will be sucked down forever, and begin to fight the downward pull.

I surface, gasping for air, and float like an otter with the sun on my face. Again I feel the fear tug at me. The fear, ever since a coloured boy drowned in the dam, that a hand might reach up out of the murky deep and touch me.

I float there, between the blue of the sky and the green of bloated faces and scaly fish.

An Egyptian goose glides across the cloudless sky.

My mind rewinds the day I went kloofing with Bach and Kala and Langtand and Flip.

We followed a river through canyons so deep that the sun only lit the black water at noon. We climbed along the river-edge rocks and jumped down waterfalls into the deep, gouged-out pools below.

Amid the yells and laughter triggered by the cold of a black-water pool, it was some time before we realised Flip was gone. When Bach eventually dived him out of the black, he was dead, just freckles and wet white flesh lolling on a rock. Flip was too dead for us to try mouth to mouth. Besides, he had scum oozing from his mouth. Bach told Kala to run like blitz with his long legs for help, although we all knew there was none for Flip van Staden.

I held Flip's rubbery hands and begged God to breathe life into him again. I hoped that Bach and Langtand would think I was just praying the kind of Catholic prayer that you see priests pray over dying heroes in films. With such prayers no one waits for the dead to leap up again. The priest just prays for the journey of the soul into the world of the dead. But my prayer was a Lazarus prayer. Every now and then I blinked my eyes open to see if Flip stirred, but his glazed eyes just stared into the sky, like the eyes of a dead fish. I heard a faint gargle as some trapped air bubbled up from his lungs.

I promised God: I will not argue politics with my father, I will skip out the sexy parts in Wilbur Smith, I will not finger through Bach's dog-eared, banned copy of *Playboy*.

But still Flip's hand flopped lifelessly.

– Forget it. He's dead, Bach said to me.

Maybe he guessed I was praying for a miracle. Afterwards, my mother said it was beautiful that I had prayed to God for poor Flip van Staden's soul. I did not tell her, or anyone, that I had not prayed for his soul, but for his life, and that God had not heard. Or, if he had, my faith was not pure enough after the *Playboy* images had become imprinted on my mind.

I shiver at the memory and swim ashore. The sand piping hot under my cold, bare feet. I run bare-assed along the dam wall to fetch my denims and tackies, keeping my eyes peeled for coloured women picking grapes in the vineyards. In the valley below, the white speck of our house, Champagne, glimmers white among the vines.

I run down the bluegum avenue again and detour through the peach orchards past La Rhône, the house of a girl called Jarrah.

For me Jarrah is the most magical word in the world. Jarrah is my bright yearning. She makes butterflies flit and dip in my mind. Sometimes she reads on the grass, in oak shadow, but she never glances up as I crunch fallen pinecones underfoot, like Tanglefoot the Red Indian.

Again I run by, again she lies under the oak, on her stomach, bare feet to the sky. Again I crunch pinecones, crack twigs, yet her head stays down, eyes glued to the book.

One day, after days and days of this Tanglefoot ritual, Zane comes home from playing with Jarrah's sister, Shanna.

– Shanna said that Jarrah said you are sooo childish always running past their house, he chirps.

– I don't care a jot, I mutter.

Just so. Tough as a cowboy. Afterwards I bury my head in my duckfeather pillow as the butterflies die.

# James Dean

Just when I think I will never ever find a girlfriend, I am invited to a dance jol in Stellenbosch over the Simonsberg mountain. I am not invited to the sokkies in Paarl. Boys like Maljan the rugby prop do not want a rooinek around when they dance with pretty Afrikaans girls with names like Annemarie and Annelise.

A girl called Tara invited me. I find Tara pretty, with her red hair twined into pigtails.

My mother drives me into Paarl in the Peugeot 404 to shop for togs in Lady Grey Street. I choose a pair of docksides, my first-ever cool shoes, after years of wearing cheap Batas to school. I also choose a red denim jacket. My mother flips up the collar, stands back.

– You remind me of James Dean, she says. You know, you are on the verge of becoming a man.

On the way home in the chugging 404, I pray to God that Tara will fall for me in my red denim jacket and docksides.

⌒

My father ferries me over the mountain to the jol in his Isuzu bakkie. The bakkie smells of cow dung and wet dog, for my father ran Nero and Fango up to the dam beforehand.

Nero and Fango are the Cape dogs. The Natal dogs died. Dingaan died of tickbite fever. My father reversed a Land Rover over Dingo. Sometimes I forget Dingaan and Dingo died. It is as if they just changed shape and live on as Nero and Fango.

When we arrive at the dance, held in an old wine cellar, Pink Floyd is chanting: *we don't need no education*. My father just shakes his head at the jarring music and Isuzus off, leaving me feeling gangly and edgy, giving off a whiff of cow dung and dog. While Pink Floyd barks at teachers to leave us kids alone, I lean against a wall, for all the world as cool as James Dean: thumbs hooked in my jean pockets.

Tara comes towards me in slow motion, red pigtails flicking, and a milky way of glitter on her forehead. She holds the hand of another guy, and as she reaches me, he pecks her on the lips. The peck, like a dog marking out his zone, is to tell me she is his. It is only then that I cotton on: she has not invited me to be with her, but just to the jol.

I want to run out and cry, but I stay in my James Dean lean and go *hi*, as if she is just another girl breezing by. Maybe this, this gaping groove furrowed out of my heart by a falling star, is how my mother felt when Cliff Richard did not have eyes for the local Durban girls in their flaring, dotty skirts.

– Have a good time, smiles Tara.

As they go, his hand snakes into her back jeans pocket.

I head for a pyramid of wine vats on the far side, hoping to hide in the murky shadows. First Jarrah and now Tara.

Maybe I will become a monk and never slide my hand into a girl's jeans.

A girl dancing alone catches my eye. She has long wispy blonde hair to her waist, and from behind you may imagine she wears nothing but her Wrangler jeans as she lilts to Fleetwood Mac.

When she turns around, though, I know she is too beautiful for me, even if Venus blinds her to the smudges of base on my face and the fat hem in my hand-me-down jeans from Lars. He is so tall that my mother has folded the hem over a few times before sewing it up, instead of just cutting off half a foot of cloth.

This time I am sure the feeling welling in me, healing me, is love. I cannot bear the thought of suffering another unconfessed love, so I walk up to her. When I reach her, the words come tumbling out:

– You remind me of a girl with long hair floating under the ice, and she's dead but she still looks beautiful and …

My words peter out. Damn, I have just told a girl fizzing with life that she looks dead.

She dips her eyebrows in a V, as if to say: Woaahh, you're weird.

– Will you dance with me, then? I plead.

She smiles at me and butterflies flutter again.

Unfortunately, just as I drift in to her, The Police begin to sing *Don't Stand So Close to Me*.

But she's so cool and just smiles at the irony and tells me her name. Alana.

I jiggle my docksides two feet away from her. Her hips seesaw before my eyes.

It turns out, I discover, that she also loved *Catcher in the Rye* and she too cried when the black boy is lost in New York in the film *e'Lollipop*.

I wish I was free to hold her the way the Afrikaans boys hold girls at their sokkies.

She does not go in for wild jiving. When a song ends she stands stock-still, glances around, waiting for the beat to kick in, or looking for better pickings.

Then, out of the blue, the deejay spins a slow song. I shuffle from foot to foot. Do I just sling my arms around her hips? I have never had my arms around a girl, never mind my hips against a girl. I hope she will give me a signal, but her eyes go all over the place, other than looking into mine.

So, I put my hands on her hips. There is a gap between her T-shirt and her jeans and I feel her skin under my hands. She turns to look deep into my eyes. We stand still as other dovetailed boys and girls float around us.

Just as I want to let go and run for it, her hipbones begin to shift under my hands. She butterflies her arms around me and dips her head on my shoulder. O God, let this dance never end and I'll promise never ever again, ever to peek at Bach's *Playboy*. I close my eyes and bury my nose in her hair. I feel her nubby breasts rub against my ribs.

Then the music is up-beat again and we begin jigging again, two feet apart.

I'm gaga about Alana. I follow her out when her father comes for her in his big white Benz. She gives me a kiss on the cheek and leaves me alone under the moon with her kiss tingling, lingering.

I stand there, catch her smell in my hands the way my father shields a match from the wind when he lights his Texans.

I hear the deep growl of my father's Isuzu. Dead on midnight. My father is always on time.

By the time my father shifts into fourth gear, the smell of cow dung and dog has chased away the traces of her scent.

– Had a good time with Tara? my father says as we swing into the corners of the Helshoogte pass.

– I hardly saw her.

– Did you dance?

– Yes, I danced.

– With the same girl, or a few girls?

– The same girl.

– Ah. I see.

He can tell I do not want to tell any more. That her name is a magic thing I want to roll around in my mouth all alone, until I am used to it.

⌒

I run up the bluegum avenue to the empty reservoir. I sit on the reservoir floor, feet folded under me, hoping the words will come to me. After a time of sitting dead still, a lizard comes out to bask. A blue dragonfly lands on my knee.

*Beloved Alana.* No. We did not go so far. A flutter of lips on my cheek does not make me her beloved.

*O Alana. I would die for you.* No. Sounds too much like *Die Stem.* At thy will to live or die, O South Africa. Dear Alana will do.

*Dear Alana*
*You are the mirage of my imagination.*

But I remember the sliding of bone under my hand. She was no mirage. Scratch it out.

*Dear Alana*
*Thoughts of you fly through my mind.*

Thoughts of you float. Thoughts of you flutter. Scratch out fly.

*Thoughts of you flutter through my mind*
*like the wings of a*

What kind of a bird? A hawk? Too wild. A dove? Too tame. A seagull. Ja.

*like the wings of a gull*
*on a sea breeze.*
*Love Gecko*

I dream of Alana day and night and wander around in a daze. My mother is cross with me for putting the Nesquik tin in the old whining Westinghouse fridge and the milk in the cupboard, so that the milk goes sour.

I forget to latch the door to the parakeet cage and the sky is flagged Caribbean blue and lime green and yellow.

The parakeets flap overhead, perch in the lemon tree, in the bluegum. They are a row of colourful pegs on Nana's washing line. Maybe their wings are too feeble after being caged for so long, or maybe they are afraid of the sudden, unwired vast sky of freedom, but they do not go far. Instead, the wild birds zone in on our yard. The butcherbirds, drongos and crows sense the tameness in the escaped parakeets and swoop at them with gaping beaks and claws.

Zane and Mila and I catch a few parakeets in a butterfly net, but the rest are pecked, till they fall to earth, flecked red and quivering to death. My mother, scared of flapping things, watches through a window. I know how it hurts her to see birds die, and I, who let them fly, dare not look into her eyes.

My father comes home with a pink envelope for me. Zane snatches it and runs out into the yard. I have no choice but to tackle him and pummel him till he lets go. I run up the avenue to the reservoir to open the bent envelope under a sinking, mother-of-pearl sun.

*Dear Gecko*
*I thought your poem was sweet. I thought you were sweet too.*
*Au revoir (that's goodbye in French)*
*Alana*
The French bit is a sign she loves me.

I want to ask Alana to see *The Gods Must be Crazy* with me at the Protea Cinema in Paarl, but I cannot see her jamming into the dung-and-dust bakkie between my father and me when she is used to a Benz. So I go on, riding the bus, running up to the dam, girlless. It is only in Wilbur Smith's novels, in Bach's tattered, fingered, taboo *Playboy* magazine, and in my dreams that I get a chance to discover girls. There is no chance of seeing them topless on the beach, as you may overseas, for the law forbids white girls to bare their nipples.

Whenever I visit Bach, I beg him to let me flick through his *Playboy* again. Forgive me God but I love to linger on the silky, butterscotch skin, the pink nipples, and the veil of hair hiding the forbidden, yearned-for, magic thing. I know guilt will gnaw at me afterwards. I know I will need to kneel in the cold, hard pews of St George's before I sip the blood of Jesus again, as the blood of Jesus may kill you just like oleander if you are in sin. I know I will not look my mother in the eyes when she serves me my supper.

Though I know all this, I still flick through the *Playboy*, my heart thudding, knowing the magazine is banned and that you can be caned if the police catch you, knowing Jesus-on-the-cross bends his head in shame.

Afterwards the images stay in my mind. A kaleidoscope of nipples and bellybuttons and parted lips. I whittle away the guilt by hurting myself. I skin my fists against the wall. I run barefoot through the orchards and vineyards (so stones and duwweltjies sting my feet), and dive deep down into the dam at night (when my fear of being sucked down into the murk is strongest). Before I go to bed, I kneel and pray to God: Dear God, save me from the women who come to me in my dreams.

But still they come. They come naked, like Botticelli's Venus, and they beg me to do things to them. They beg me to tip Peel's honey into their bellybuttons and lick it out. They beg me to drip a drop of the blood of a pigeon on their forehead. They beg me to sniff at their bottoms, as if I am a dog. But when I want to peck at their hips, they titter at my puny, puppy cock.

# killing Biko

As girls stay at bay, there is time for other things. I watch Bach shoot frogs in the dam. The shot frogs flip over onto their backs, tongues of white in the dark water. I go pigeon-hunting with Bach and Lars. Lars shoots them out of the pines with his .22. The pigeons flap to earth, a frenzy of feathers. It is my job to run up to the jerking bird and tug its head off with a quick twist. We pluck the birds, kebab them on wire to cook on a fire under the stars with the hiss of burning vinestumps and the hum of motorcars along the sawmill road and the shrill cry of guineafowl in the bluegums.

Lars has a pig called Steely Dan that thinks he is a dog. Neglected by his mother, Steely Dan was rescued by Lars's father and given to their dog, Hella, who was in milk. So Steely Dan sucked dog milk from Hella with her pups, Fidel and Marx. He always comes bounding out with Fidel and Marx to bark at coloureds who run the gauntlet of Nero and Fango on one side of the avenue, and Fidel and Marx and Steely Dan on the other.

Just like a dog, Steely Dan digs down on a blazing day to lie in the cool unearthed sand below. Just like a dog, Steely Dan edges so close to the vinestump fire that stray coals singe his skin. It is around the fire with the dogs and Steely Dan and the kebabbed pigeons that Lars tells Bach and me about the police and the way that they killed Steve Biko.

– After being fucked around by the SB, the secret police, they chucked him half-dead in the back of a van and drove him from Port Elizabeth to Pretoria over dirt roads. The police said Biko starved himself to death, of his own free will. Bastards. Truth is, he died of a bleeding brain.

As the sparks firefly into the sky, I find it hard to believe such a thing can happen in South Africa, my country.

– Thing is, it all came out when this journalist dude, Donald Woods, fled to England with photos of Biko's fucked-up body. And each time a man dies, the police tell another story: He hanged himself in his cell with his bootlaces. He fell from a high window.

*A man's skull cracking open against the tar, like a crab's shell.*

– He fell down the stairs.

(Farmboy on Christmas trips to bigtown Pietermaritzburg: I cling to my mother's skirt, scared of catching my fingers in the steel comb teeth of the rolling steps.)

– He slipped on a bar of soap in the shower.

Slip on the Lifebuoy. Slip on the Sunlight. Another way to die in the Cape.

# memento

Until now I have just hunted lizards, birds and frogs on the farm, but now my hunter uncle has invited us to go hunting big game in Botswana. After two days caged in the old 404, I am now on the back of my uncle's Ford 4x4. The 4x4 bucks and keels as it plunges through the thorn bundu. There's a skinner on the back with us and a Bushman tracker on the roof.

The Ford jams to a halt, and I am flung onto my hands and knees, cracking the lens of my binoculars. My father's strong hand tugs me to my feet.

A kudu bull stands focused in my one-eyed binoculars, so dignified with his spiral horns and pinstriped coat. He has a white line across the bridge of his nose, as if he's wearing reading glasses.

A gunshot bangs in my ear, echoes *kadow wow wow wow*. Smoke whispers from the barrel of my uncle's gun. The Ford crashes through bundu after the wounded kudu. The Bushman tracker clings to the roof, like a baby monkey riding its mother, his eyes skinned for traces of the blood spoor. He dangles a stick over the windshield to signpost the way for the driver below.

The kudu lies dead in the dust. Blood trickles from his mouth and clots in the sand.

Vultures loop in the sky above.

The hot bullet that the skinner digs out of the kudu's neck is in my hand.

– A memento of your first hunt, my uncle says.

A spot of blood stays on my palm after I slip the bullet into my pocket. I look on as the skinner peels the kudu. The tracker chops off his horns with an axe. Another memento.

The campfire: a gathering around the coals while the kudu liver sizzles on a spade.

– A delicacy, they tell me amid laughter and beer and meat strung up in a baobab and the *yip yip yip* of a hyena.

# pennywhistle

As Lars is freelancing for *The Cape Times*, he sometimes goes into the black townships to *cruise for news*, as he puts it. Lars reckons, since I just turned sixteen, I ought to go backstage: see the real, raw-boned South Africa. I clamber into his rusty old VW beetle, called Dirt. The road bridging the familiar, mapped-out world of my childhood and the alien, other Africa becomes rutted as the tar gives out.

– It will be surreal for you but don't be scared, laughs Lars.

I imagine I am about to enter a world in which houses, chimneys and dogs melt, as if in a Salvador Dali painting. I am on edge, but Lars is as cool as Cool Hand Luke. As long as Lars is around I will be okay.

Dirt rides a pot-holed road through the brick matchbox houses of Jamaica Township, one like the other. There are no palms. No trees of any kind. Just solitary, moth-orbited lamps. Then the brick houses give way to tumbledown shacks in unlamped dark, and they do melt into one another. Dirt goes on, further and further into this jumbled maze, dodging deep dongas to keep from turtling over.

Blanketed silhouettes huddle around glowing drums. Firefly sparks dart starward.

Bony dogs slink into hovering shadows.

A man in a Che Guevara beret and a moth-eaten grey blanket leaps into the headlights, swinging a long-bladed panga over his head like a Samurai.

Dirt jams to a halt. Lars winds down the window.

– No fear, Comrades. I guard your car with my life, Che calls, jabbing the long blade at a mangy dog squirting pee at Dirt's hubcap.

The dog yelps and flees.

I imagine we will return to find Dirt strewn with the corpses of dogs and men who venture within panga range.

I follow Lars, finger hooked through a loop of his Levi's, along a mud alleyway winding among shacks of zinc, plank and paraffin tin. Sounds of radio jazz and distant barking and murmurs mingle. The shacks ooze smells of bubbling pap and sour beer and Vaseline.

Doors ajar cast winking images:

A family huddles around paraffin stoves.

A mother gives her child her breast.

Another woman washboards clothes in a tin tub.

Old men play cards in dim candlelight, slapping them down like children playing snap.

An open-mouthed child stands in a doorway and stares at two white phantoms drifting through his world.

Another door frees a gush of beer fumes, smoke and pounding music. White teeth draw us, brothers and comrades, into the crowd. Figures filter through the walls until it is steamy inside. I smile at all faces my eyes zoom in on, for the panga still slices through my mind. Besides, Lars has gone out of sight.

A man called Matanga, who reeks of Brylcreem and beer, corners me. He tells me of his girlfriend's unfaithfulness.

– She kissed a coloured from Salt River. On the lips.

Matanga is so close I feel his spit speck my face.

– The bitch I wanted to marry.

I shake my head.

Matanga pulls a gun out of his pocket.

– I'll kill her.

He morbidly studies his gun.

– You don't have to kill her, I mumble.

– Whajusay?

– Do you *have* to kill her?

Matanga leans even closer and whispers:

–You don't feel my hurt.

I resist the urge to wipe my face free of spit.

Throughout my dialogue with Matanga, I keep shuffling to jazzy music. If my feet stand still for a minute, some bopping dude zooms in on me, tunes me to *relaaax*. But it is hard to relax with Matanga in a morbid mood. He swigs down one Lion beer after another and sinks deeper in his blues.

– My fortune gone on a ring.

He shakes his head, peers into his Lion.

Then, out of the blue, he cheers up, asks me to dance. He still has his gun in his pants, so I follow him into the tangle of dancers.

We dance, Matanga and I, to a zippy bigband song, full of tsotsi, cocky trumpets chasing a scared pennywhistle.

Then Matanga goes out to pee Lion beer.

I shrink into a corner, eyes skinned for Lars. But he is nowhere.

Giggling girls tug me out of my corner and draw me into their ring to mimic their Soweto jitterbug jive. They laugh at the sight of a white boy making a jerky bid to mimic African rhythm. One girl with white white teeth wiggles her shoulders so her dungareed breasts bobble and jiggle two inches away from my face. Her nipples peek out, then tuck in again.

– Viva Mandelaaa, cries a woman in a black turban, as if drowning in the sea of smoke.

Fists dart up like cobra heads to a chorus of *Viva Mandela, viva Mandela.*

– Amandla, the turbanned woman cries.

– Awetu, the dancers chant.

Fists fly high. I lift my white fist in a shy black-power salute.

– MK is coming, calls a schoolboy armed with a plank AK47.

– MK is coming, I echo.

I have no idea who MK is.

Just as I catch sight of Matanga bearing down on me again, I feel Lars's firm hand draw me through the crowd and into the cool night.

– I juiced my info for a story. Vamoose.

Dirt is an albino hippo under the moon. Che kips behind the wheel, the panga on the dash. He jolts awake when Lars taps on the window. He swings the door and *Lola* escapes from the radio and *la la la lolas* up to the moon.

Dirt drops Che in the rearview, rattles over the pot-holed roads, hums along the tar.

– Who's MK, Lars?

– Umkhonto weSizwe. The Spear of the Nation. They are the underground soldiers of the ANC.

I picture the plankgun boy running along tunnels under the earth.

– You seemed to enjoy yourself with the girls, Lars jokes.

– Come on, I deny.

But the dungareed breasts jiggle on in my mind as the moon follows Dirt home.

# the outsider

I have moved out of our thatched Dutch house into the maid's room, under the same zinc roof as the Peugeot 404. I paint the walls yellow. I pin up a ragged, dog-eared Dylan I begged Lars for. I feel independent here, though I go back into the house for my mother's cooking and to bath.

One night as I come to the back door, a rat darts out of the cat hole cut for Lalapanzi, and scratches up my leg. I yell and my father runs out with his .22, expecting to find me dead in my bed.

Another time, I see a puffadder slither across the path that leads from my room to the back door.

Another way to die in the Cape.

If you survive the falling bluegum, the invading Russians and the deadly oleander, if you dodge bulls and sidestep bars of soap, you stand a good chance of being fanged to death.

⟡

Zane begs me to play cricket when I want to be alone in the murk of my outside room with Camus and Dylan. He thuds a ball against the wall until I give in.

Today, Zane just stands at the door until I look up from *The Outsider*.

– Hey Zane, you OK? I say, my mind still on the beach with Meursault and his girl Marie.

Meursault and Marie drink the sea foam and spurt it up at the sky. Meursault's mouth burns with the bitterness of the salt. I know the taste of burning saltwater on my tongue. This scene with Marie, her face suntanned like a flower, is good. Till this moment the story is dull.

– I dunno bro, mumbles Zane. I had this dream. You remember the way the big girls on the bus sat me on their lap 'coz of my blue eyes?

– And the 50 cents you got for ice-cream if you let them comb your hair like a rabbit, I tease.

He giggles.

– Hey bro, you ever see a girl naked?

– Naked? No. Lars tells me in Denmark the girls tan with no bikini top on. And in Amsterdam they sit naked in the windows.

– No way.

– I tell you it's true.

– Do you think we will ever go as far as Denmark, or Amsterdam?

– I hope so. If we go, Country Joe, don't forget the Fish.

We cycle through the orchards behind Boschendal, where the geese hiss at us and chickens dart away to hide among the bamboo. Over the Dwars River. Past the coloured school. The afternoon kids at their desks stare dreamily out of the windows at the morning kids larking in the yard. There are too few desks and teachers for all the coloured kids of the valley to have morning school.

We play tennis in shorts and tackies on the sand court of

the Groot Drakenstein Games Club which the coloured barman rolls flat and hard. Between sets we dive into the frog-green pool.

⤔

Bach bore the flak of hanging around at Paarl Boys' High with an outsider like me. Maljan and the boys called him my nanny.

– I don't give a damn, Bach said to me.

He imagined he was Steve McQueen. Nothing would faze him. Nothing ripple his cool.

While Bach was around, no one dared touch me. Bach was as big as Maljan, the rugby prop, and Visoog Vorster was cross with him for playing football at the club in Paarl rather than playing rugby for the school. Visoog Vorster loved to mock how football players dived whenever a boot skimmed their shin, the way they hugged and kissed after scoring a goal, *like homos.*

The rugby boys around us guffawed and winked at Bach, who everyone knew was a footballer.

– I don't give a damn, Bach would mutter.

Then his folks sent him to boarding school in Pretoria, because of the shame. One night he was caught swimming naked with a girl in the school pool after a dance. Visoog Vorster wanted to cane him, but Bach would not bend. So he was kicked out instead. Not to bend for Visoog Vorster was the bravest thing I had ever heard of. Bach begged not to be sent north but his folks said the skinny dip at school was the last straw.

He cried at the station in Paarl. It was the first time I saw him lose his cool. As the train pulled away, he called out to me:

– Don't let the bastards get you down.

Now Bach is gone, and Lars is away most of the time, dodging his army call-up, foraying into the townships. The police called on his folks but they said they hadn't seen him for a while. The police filled a cardboard box with his university notes and paper-back novels, margins graffitied with his thoughts and the scores of Leeds United games.

When he comes back to the farm, Lars parks Dirt in the vine-yards. When you hear Fidel and Marx whine, you know he is out there, in the dark, weaving through the vines.

~

My history teacher, Captain Malan, used to be an undercover policeman. He ought not to go by his title, but he enjoys the boys calling him Captain. He tells us it is natural, the ladder of race in South Africa.

– Blacks were cursed by God to be hewers of wood, to work the land for the whites. Therefore they have not evolved at the same pace.

I put up my hand.

– But, Captain, if blacks have not evolved as fast, then how-come they run faster, jump further and box harder?

Captain Malan taps his head.

– Fact is, we outwitted them, he smirks.

The class laughs at his wit.

~

During break, in the lee of the pump house by the school pool, I read books Lars lends me, like *Death in Venice* or *Dangling Man*. Sometimes it is lonely there in my outcast corner of the school. The loneliness began slowly: a whisper of kaffirboetie, niggerlover, a jolt in a crowd, a bag of schoolbooks dropped down a stairwell onto my head.

Today I read *Waiting for Godot* while I chew an avocado sandwich my mother made for me. I cannot focus on *Godot*. I rewind the history lesson we just had. I wish I had thought of a reply to Captain Malan's smug punch line: We outwitted them. I see now, in hindsight, how I played into his hands by focusing on the physical. I wish I had had a black poet, or novelist, at my fingertips. We read Wordsworth and Blake and all the English poets. We read Golding and Paton and Hemingway, and other white writers, but I have never read a word written by a black man.

I discover I have turned the page. My eyes had gone on skimming the lines though my mind was not on the play. I do not worry to rewind, for Gogo and Didi are still waiting under the same dry tree. A shadow falls across the page. I squint up to see Maljan, eclipsing the sun. He is flanked by the De Beer brothers. Behind them, in silhouette, a scrum of other boys from my class.

– Hey Gecko, we've had it with this kaffir-lover shit of yours.

– Le's just beat the hell out of the kaffirboetie, chorus the De Beer brothers.

Maljan and the De Beer brothers pin me down and stuff avocado sandwich into my mouth. They laugh at my bulging hamster cheeks. A hand pinches my nose so I cannot breathe at all. I writhe under their nobbly knees and bony fists. Frantic for air, I spew avocado on their blue school shirts. The laughing dies.

– Let's just beat the hell out of the kaffirboetie, go the De Beer brothers again.

But Maljan has other ideas and pulls out a red Swiss Army knife.

– You have to learn that you can't just run around thinking you are Gandhi.

He folds out the corkscrew, twists his wrist, as if screwing it into a cork, or skin, then folds it back in. Then he flicks out the knife blade.

– You forget this black shit, you hear?

Maljan grasps a handful of hair like a Red Indian about to scalp me. He hacks out a gaping, ragged hole.

– Now there is no nanny to come running.

He walks to the edge of the pool and scatters my hair over the surface of the water. Then they go. My hair floats for a long time while I rub the threadbare hole at the back of my head.

In the mirror in the toilets, it looks as if my barber had a jitter fit.

Head buried under my blazer, I ride out the sniggers on the bus.

Back on the farm, my mother is furious.

– I'm going to call up the headmaster. This has gone too far.

I beg her not to, as I know it will make my life unbearable at school if I am called a kaffirboetie and a rat too.

# bikini

I see Jarrah at the games club. She suns by the pool in a pink bikini on a sky-blue towel. Her blond hair is tinted creamsoda green by the chlorine. By now I know she thinks me childish, so I do not bother to butterfly up and down the pool. She unhooks her bikini top while she lies reading on her tummy. Zane dives in and cold drops of water rain on her back. She flinches, giving me an eyeful of forbidden skin, untouched by the sun.

# red rover

Physical Training at Paarl Boys': barefoot, shirtless boys in white shorts spinning out the rugby ball on the field below the white school facade and the row of ancient oaks. Weaving, dipping, diving, shying the hands that fly after you. Flicking the ball out, to left or right, just before a hand touches you.

Afterwards, I gasp as the icy shower water stings my grass burns.

I become aware of a sinister stillness and wonder how long I have been alone. I turn the tap and reach for my towel, to discover it is gone. Instinctively, I cover my balls with my hands. At that moment Maljan comes around the corner. He fills his six foot four with a cocksure, cowboy machismo. His long arms fall lazily, in a John Wayne way.

– Red rover, red rover, run over, he taunts.

My heart bongoes against my rib cage as I go past him.

I feel relief. His taunt was just bravado. But then, the sting of a flat, fanned hand across my back. I flinch, but still face forwards, sensing his desire to hurt. To turn around is to fetch a fist in my teeth, so I go on up the steps to the benches where the clothes hang on steel hooks.

The other boys from my class stare ahead of them like zombies as they tie their ties and laces.

From behind my flaming back Maljan hisses:

– Pretty white ass you got there, for a kaffirboetie.

Still wet, I pull on my Jockeys. I am buttoning up my shirt when he thrusts me against the wall. A steel hook stabs me in the forehead. I fall to my knees on the cold floor, as if at the altar rail. I finger my forehead, gingerly. My fingers come away filmed in blood.

Reaching for the hook, I pull myself to my feet. Blood dams in my eyebrows, drips into my eyes. I turn to face Maljan.

– Listen, Jan. I don't want to fight with you.

– You don't wanna fight hey? But I wanna fuck you up, you kaffirboetie. Your tutumandela shit makes me vomit, you know.

He gobs up the slime from his gullet and spits at me.

I wipe blood and gob out of my eyes.

– Mandela Mandela monkeydela, he mocks.

The other boys act is if they see no evil. At Paarl Boys' High you stay out of a fight.

Maljan jabs me hard in the ribs to provoke some resistance.

– If you believe all this tutumandela shit, why don't you stan' up and fight for it, hey? You too much a moffie, hey?

I stand there, head bent, holding my balls. Just then the bell goes.

– You fuckin' moffie. Maljan's parting shot as he follows the other boys out, my grey school shorts in hand.

☞

Our next class is with Baldhead Bosman who canes boys who come late. Even Maljan is scared of him. Baldhead Bosman, who vivisects rabbits with the same cheer as he canes boys. He makes us study the squirming guts of the rabbit, clear as cogs in a defaced clock. Baldhead Bosman, who believes in plum.

– Let me tell you boys, there is nothing like your plum for growing a good stick. I have tried out peach and pear, but I always come back to plum.

I arrive late and bleary-eyed in white shorts between my striped blazer and grey socks. He tells me to bend. I bend over his desk. Under my nose, mice scurry through the sawdust of their cage. He jacks me with his plum and I jerk up as it stings.

– Boys, there are some facts you can verify through experiment. One such fact is the pliancy of plum.

Cawing laughter comes from the tiered desks.

Again the plum swishes through the air. Again I jump up.

Again the boys laugh. It is hard not to laugh at the sight of a boy being caned. The jackknifing over the desk, the jack-in-the-box jumping up to rub ass.

– So the kaffirboetie is a highjumper, hey?

I stand in front of him, rubbing ass.

– The boys tell me you would let Mandela go.

– Yes, sir.

– You're out of your head, my boy. If communists such as Mandela are free to run around, then this country is lost. You hear?

I just hang my head.

– You're not to blame, boy. I like your spirit. It's the cunning English papers that put subversive thoughts in your head. Is it not?

– Maybe, Sir.

– I thought so. Sit down, my boy.

At break I see boys on the rugby field staring up at my grey shorts flapping in the wind atop a rugby post as high as a yacht's mast. I stand forlorn on the edge of the field amid wild whistling and yahooing.

Then, out of the blue, Fanie Viljoen, a boy from my class, tugs off his shoes, peels off his socks, and begins to climb the rugby post. The yahooing boys jeer him, hurl orange peels at him, but he climbs on upwards, like an islander shinning up a coconut palm. The post begins to sway but Fanie Viljoen inches up higher and higher towards my shorts.

Boys chant: Moffie moffie moffie moffie …

In the school they say Fanie Viljoen is a homo because he goes for rides with Mister Sands to the Strand for ice-cream. I once asked Bach what a homo was and he said: A guy who sucks another guy's cock. Oh, I said.

I wonder why my mother and father never tell me such things. Sex is a taboo word in our house, but my mother did once give me D.H. Lawrence to read. Like a needle caught in a record groove, I lingered on the part where the gamekeeper puts forget-me-nots in the woman's maidenhair. I love the word maidenhair for a girl's love hair. It conjures up a mystic image of hair flowing lazy as seagrass under water.

While Fanie Viljoen climbs up the rugby post I find I do not care a jot if he goes for rides with Mister Sands. All I know is he braves the jeers and the orange peels and runs the risk of being beaten up by Maljan just for me, rooinek kaffirboetie. We are moffies together, Fanie and I. Fanie because he rides with Mister Sands, and me because Maljan made me cry, because I read books instead of playing touch rugby at break, because I play hockey, because I do not fight back.

Fanie Viljoen reaches for my pants while the pole sways and,

instead of dropping them, drapes them over his head before sliding down. When his bare feet touch the grass, he walks over with
my shorts, my shame, in his hands and casually flicks them to me.
Boys wolf-whistle as if a girl breezed by.

# fee fi fo fum

– The headmaster wants to see you, Baldhead Bosman tells me. Regarding subversive thoughts. I'm sorry, but I felt it my duty.

I recall Stompie's striped ass, and I reel as I stand up. I feel the eyes of my class bore into me. I stumble as I go out, and Maljan laughs. Bosman hits him over the head with the spine of a book.

The school was never so dark and cold. I want to run for it, thumb a ride to Cape Town harbour, and jump on a cargo ship bound for England. England, where teachers do not beat boys and where, as Grandpa Barter tells it, you may stand on a tomato box in Hyde Park and say the queen is daft without even the pigeons bothering to flutter.

Visoog Vorster's door looms in front of me. I *tok tok*, tentatively.

I hear a bass rumble. I open the door to the room steeped in myth. Sure enough, there is the row of bamboo canes on top of the cupboard. My ass tingles at the mere sight of them.

On the desk a platoon of fountain pens stands at attention. Visoog Vorster's face looms through a cloud of cigar smoke.

– Mister Bosman sent you?

– Yes, sir.

– You've been sent to me before?

– No, sir.

– A first offence. I have heard from Mister Bosman that your head is full of politics.

He spits out the word politics. He makes it sound as if my head is teeming with vermin.

– No, sir. Not just politics, sir.

There are the ass-wagging women in Bach's *Playboy* who weave their way into my dreams. There is the daydream of being a writer, like Hemingway, or Wilbur Smith. There is the wish to be as long and lithe as Lars is. There is the yearning to see my Grandpa's England, where you eat fish and chips out of a newspaper. But I can tell none of this to Visoog Vorster, who wants my head full of chalk and rugby.

– Come now, if I let you off this time, will you rid your head of such nonsense? You're here to enjoy school, not carry the world on your shoulders, you know.

For a moment the deal he offers is sweet. I get off scot-free and all I have to do is forget. Forget Biko's bleeding head. Forget Mandela behind bars, time grooving furrows in his forehead. Forget the fallen pomegranate heads, oozing red juice on pavements.

– I'm not sure I can just forget, sir.

– Well, I'm sorry, but in that case you'll have to bend.

He stands up, dwarfing me. I imagine he will cry: *Fee fi fo fum, I smell the blood of an Englishman.* Instead, as if offering me a range of lollipops:

– Which cane shall I use?

– I don't know, sir.

All the canes look as if they will sting hard.

– Well then, I'll choose for you.

He reaches for a long cane and bends it, head to tail. Then he swings a few mock lashes in the air. *Swish, swish, swish* goes the cane.

My teeth jibber. My knees jelly.

– Four cuts. And to think you might have walked.

Visoog Vorster smiles tobacco-yellowed fangs as I, unbidden, drag my feet to his desk and bend over it. It confirms the fame of his method, means he will not have to teach me my part in this ritual.

My shorts pull taut across my ass. I wait for the swish of the cane. When it comes, I gasp.

The sting is worse than a wasp sting. It is like being stung by a jellyfish, and the sting of a jellyfish can make a man cry. It is like all the times I grazed the skin off my knees, in one searing rip.

And then there is the gap.

The gap when time chewing-gums out as I wait for the next cut and fight the instinct to rub my ass, or to cry. Lars told me, crying just makes Visoog Vorster cane harder.

The next cut falls on the same raw, raging place.

– Oh, Jeeezuz, I cry out as I grab my ass.

Visoog Vorster prises my fingers away with the cane, as you might poke at a baboon spider or a scorpion with a stick.

– No rubbing. And do not bandy the name of the Lord about.

I bend again and clutch at the far rim of his desk.

The third cut falls on fresh skin. I somehow cling to the desk to keep my fingers from flying to my flaring ass.

– Good, says Visoog Vorster. I am not fond of melodrama.

The last cut falls on wounded skin. I shoot up, loosing a banshee yell: *yaai yaai yaai.* I hop from foot to foot.

Visoog Vorster slides the cane home among the other canes. He squints out of the window onto the rugby field, giving me time to stop hopping and sobbing. Then he turns to face me.

– Now, you forget this liberal nonsense. You hear?

I wipe my dangling snot on my sleeve.

He reaches out his hand, as if to say: no hard feelings. The shaking of hands is, by tradition, the last act of the ritual of branding kudu stripes across a boy's ass.

# panama hat

One break Baldhead Bosman's classroom is left unlocked. I steal inside and climb the high bookshelf ladder to see what secrets the out-of-reach volumes hide. On the top shelf I find fingerprints on the dusty spine of *The Voyage of the Beagle*. I slide it out. As the book falls open, a paper drops out and wings down to the floor. I climb down, heart beating hard, for Baldhead Bosman will kill me if he catches me red-handed.

The paper is a black-and-white photograph of a coffee-skinned woman on beach sand. She lies with her legs Y-ed open. She squeezes a breast with one hand. With the other, she holds a Coca-Cola bottle down there. Half of the bottle is in her.

I wonder why Bosman has a photograph of a Coca-Cola bottle inside a coloured or Caribbean woman inside Darwin when he is forever ranting on about the coloureds and the kaffirs wanting their hands on what the whites have and that one day it will be us and them and that if we do not learn hard it will be us down the mines and behind the plough and them sitting on the veranda with a cigar and coffee and brandy.

I feel sexy, so I pocket the photo.

Leon du Plessis and I work the projector when flicks, usually James Bond or Clint Eastwood, are shown in the hall on the last day of term. He is the film fundi. I just hand him the reels. Still, I love the dark of the projection room, where I can watch films, unseen and undisturbed by Maljan and the De Beer brothers. Leon and I play in the Boland hockey team. He is the one who shoots the goals. He dreams of being a fighter pilot. Me, I still dream of going overseas, of seeing the world, maybe writing a novel, one day.

I regret confessing to my father that I want to be a writer. He laughs.

– You're always in your own little dream world, of writers and explorers. Maybe I should send you to Sunflower Home.

Sunflower Home is a home for daft kids, like Spud. I know he does not mean it, but it is true that I am a bit daft. I spill my milk as if I am a dribbling old madman, I burn toast, I toss my dirty socks in the dustbin, I let the bath overflow.

Almost every night at supper my father says:

– How many times must I tell you not to stick your knife in your mouth? One day you'll cut your tongue off.

It drives him mad.

There is a *tok tok* at the door of the projection room. It is Mister Sands. He tells Leon he wants to talk to me alone. My heart beats because of the rumours of the rides for ice-cream. He just stands there in the flickering light, for a long time.

– I heard about your being caned. He's a bastard, is Vorster.

I shrug, though I am amazed by his risky words.

– I share your misgivings about South Africa, he goes on, but this isn't a free country where you can just mouth what you feel.

He steps forward, rests chalkdust fingertips on my shoulder.

– I'm sorry about the cane. If you have such restless thoughts, about Mandela, about injustice, you can always come and talk to me. You hear?

I nod. As I nod, I pray he will not want to go for an ice-cream with me.

He winks at me, then turns on his heels.

His fingers leave dusty afterthoughts on my blue school shirt.

There is another teacher at Paarl Boys' High who stands out from the rest. Mister Slater, my English teacher, wears a panama hat and he never canes us. His words mesmerise me, like the tones from a snakecharmer's flute. Under Mister Slater, I discover words have individual character and history, that *flamboyant* comes from the French for *aflame*, that *window* comes from the Nordic *vindauge*, wind eye.

Mister Slater tells us of Jung and other heroes: of how Oedipus wanted to outfoot his fate yet ran toward it, of how Odysseus out-witted the Trojans with a hollow horse, of the sirens who lured men to their death on the rocks. He weaves together mythology and adventure and hints of the unexplored world of romance. He reads us the part in *The Grapes of Wrath*, ripped out of the school library copy, about the priest who loves the girls.

– Censoring a book is a vandalising of art. Such people ought to be fed to the crocodiles.

After school Mister Slater crosses the rugby field to his Zephyr under the jacarandas, unlocks the boot and drops his panama hat into it before going round to the driver's door to climb in. Pukka English.

There is a boy in my English class we all call Slimjan. There is Maljan the mad Jan, and Slimjan the clever Jan. He is so sharp at untangling metaphor and finding motifs for Mister Slater that I am bitterly jealous of him. He can track images filtering through strands of narrative like a Bushman picking up the blood spoor with his hawk eye. A drop of blood in dry grass. A bent twig. A hoof dint in the sand.

I want to beat Slimjan in English; after all I am the rooinek whose grandpa went to Oxford, and here is this boer boy with an uncanny flair for writing. Mister Slater says he is inspired by the muses. I wish Mister Slater would find my writing inspired, but he always writes in the margin:

*Too pedestrian.*

My writing walks, or plods, instead of flying like Slimjan's.

Or: *Too literal.*

I have to unwind, let my imagination freewheel. But it is hard to unwind with Maljan wanting to beat the *tutumandela shit* out of me and Baldhead Bosman forever flexing his plum and the De Beer brothers lurking like wolves in the back of my mind.

For me South Africa is inescapably literal. As literal as a cane biting into flesh, as a steel hook in the head.

# kissing Jade

After Grandpa Rudd died from falling out of a coral tree, Granny came to live in the Cape. She has a house in Windermere Road, Muizenberg, near Zandvlei. During the school holidays I go and stay with her.

On the way to Muizenberg, I always spend the day in Cape Town.

My father drops me at Klapmuts station, on the line from Paarl to Cape Town.

The train whistles and wheezes through the Klapmuts vineyards, then the Muldersvlei cow fields, then the northern suburbs' backyards with their colourful washing and barking dogs.

An hour later the train arrives in Cape Town. Ahead, under its cloth of cloud, Table Mountain looks down on the city and the harbour of moored cargo ships and yachts and the seagull bay and Robben Island.

How many years does it take for jail bars to rust through in the sea wind? I wonder.

From the station I step into Town, a carnival of colour and sound.

Muslim men in tasselled flowerpot hats and Muslim women hidden behind black cloth. Coloured flowersellers with bright cloths on their heads, selling proteas and roses. Magazine stalls. Fruitsellers calling: peachaaas and lichiiis and bananaaas.

Amid the honking taxis and buskers and double-deckers of Adderley Street, Jan van Riebeeck stands unruffled, casting his stone gaze mountainwards.

I haunt the backstreet bookshops and choose something with an arty cover that catches my eye, and a morbid title that Lars would give the nod to: *As I Lay Dying*, *Heart of Darkness*, *Hunger*.

I walk down St George's Street and listen to a banjoman or watch a tapdancer. Superstitiously, I drop a coin in a hat and head for the cheap and dark Black Dog Café. As I sit there waiting for my Coke float to arrive, Leonard Cohen sings *So Long, Marianne*. I dip my nose into my new paperback and breathe in the smell of a virgin book, its spine uncracked and its mystery unspilt. Outside a bergie hustles folk for a few cents.

The best thing after lunch in town is a film. Somehow I can forget my Paarl Boys' blues when the screen images begin to roll and I dig into a box of hot popcorn.

I enjoy the cigarette ads. The rugged Camel guy pontooning his Land Rover across crocodile torrents and rigging a tent in tropical downpours, then sparking up a Camel to the distant call of a fish eagle. The Winston ads: a festival of rodeo cowboys, Colorado rapids, California bikinis, neon-pink lips swigging Coca-Cola.

At the end of a film I stay as the credits unreel. Not to discover who the gaffer and keygrip are, so much as to linger in the magic before surfacing to the real world.

Afterwards I catch a train out to Muizenberg and Granny Rudd.

Rondebosch. Newlands. Wynberg. Plumstead. Retreat. Lakeside. Muizenberg.

Though Lakeside is closer to Zandvlei, where windsurfers skim across the lagoon, and the house in Windermere Road, I always go on to Muizenberg station. From there I walk along Muizenberg beach in the cold tangy wind off False Bay. Across False Bay, towards the Hottentots Holland Mountains, I can just make out the Strand and the harbour of Gordon's Bay on the far curve.

Granny Rudd has somehow come to life since Grandpa died. We drink the red wines he had stored away for his rockingchair days. We play scrabble late into the night while Grandpa's Miles Davis records fizz under the needle and the sea wind rattles the window and Granny tells me again about the jacaranda days in Durban. She tells me she loved another man before she met Grandpa, but there was a rumour he had coloured blood in his family and her mother forbade her to see him again.

– Now that Grandpa is dead, I sometimes think of my first love again. Strange, isn't it? That I still feel like a girl sometimes.

She laughs. I find it unsettling to think of a girl, with a girl's thoughts and desires, hiding inside her sagging frame, but I smile at her anyway.

During the day, in Muizenberg, I walk along Sunrise Beach to watch the oilskinned fishermen hauling in seagull-plagued nets. Sometimes sharks are caught in the nets and, mesmerised by their cold eyes and rippling gills, I prod at a sack of teeth and muscle with my toe.

At sunset I run along the coastal road, a road echoed by the railway that twists like a centipede over the rocks to Simonstown. I run past the red and yellow and blue and green cabins at St James' tidal pool. Past the vividly painted fishing boats in Kalk Bay, where they used to hunt whales in the old days, where coloured boys handline from the harbour wall, dangling bare toes like shark bait over the waves.

Far beyond the handlining boys the lights of Simonstown string out like beads in the falling dusk.

I run along the beach under a half moon, reflected in the wave foam. Ahead I see figures huddled around a driftwood fire. The sound of a guitar on the breeze and the amber flicker of the fire on their faces draw me to them.

A girl strums the guitar, sings Bob Marley over the cadences of the sea. I linger at the edge of the pool of firelight to let her voice flow through me. A young man, aware of me there, half in the dark, shifts up to make a gap in the ring for me. So I sit down in the sand, feel the breeze cool the sweat on my skin and sip at this new wine of being with folk who are young and free and smile at me.

I stare at the girl with the guitar as she sits across from me in her frayed denim shorts, so short that I glimpse her lime-green panties as she plays. Her long black hair catches the firelight in glints and hints, merges with the sliver of shadow in the shallow valley between her breasts. She rocks as she sings so the cotton spanning her breasts goes taut, then slack, then taut again, like a sail catching a sulky breeze.

When she lays the guitar aside and hugs her knees I still see a hint of lime.

Words about freedom and injustice ripple around. They laugh at the thought of Sha Na Na being at Woodstock with true soul poets: Joplin and Hendrix. One guy tunes that Kerouac wrote *On the Road* in three weeks on one long unravelling bog roll. They squabble over whether *Ulysses* is literature, or shit. The guitargirl tells them how cool it is in London and Amsterdam. They are in awe of her, for she has been there, *overseas*.

– Amsterdam is coffeeshop mecca, and London club mecca. South Africa is just so … out of time.

Then she turns to me.

– Where are you from?

I do not want to tell her I am a farmboy from Groot Drakenstein.

– Paarl, I fib.

But any place out that way, in the Boland, is primitive to folks from Cape Town.

– So, do you go to Stellenbosch University? she digs.

– I'm still at school, at Paarl Boys' High.

– Isn't that where they still have initiation and all that primal ritual?

I nod. No doubt they all went to larney private schools in Cape Town.

She comes over to sit by me, and butterflies flap in my stomach.

– I'm Jade. My mother was a flowerchild. Called me Jade River. Cool, hey?

– I'm Gecko.

– Cool name. You also a flowerchild baby?

– No. It's just a name I picked up in Zululand.

– Zululand. Far out. Teach me some words.

– Inyoka is snake. Inja is a dog.

She echoes the words and the others laugh.

– I dig ethnic words. They sound so instinctive. I study music at UCT, first year. It's so bohemian after the discipline of school.

– You ever meet a Danish guy called Lars? He's my friend. He studied at UCT.

– No. UCT's a labyrinth. It's not like a school out in Paarl, you know.

Fool farmboy for imagining she would know Lars. Though he writes freelance for *The Cape Times*, he never gets a byline. That honour is for the big guns.

– I can't get over you being in such a savage school.

I tell her about mad Maljan and the hounding De Beer brothers, about Visoog Vorster's run-up and Baldhead Bosman's love for plum. As I tell her these things we drink red wine, cheap Tassenberg from a box. She squeezes my hand, stares mesmerised eyes deep into mine, as if I am a traveller from another world.

The fire burns down to a glow. The others go, now two, now one, until it is just Jade and me, alone on Muizenberg beach. Jade holds my hand and I follow her behind the beach cabins. We lie down together on the sand that collects there in deep drifts.

– Perhaps the police will toss me in jail for kissing a schoolboy, Jade jokes.

As my lips touch hers, gingerly, I imagine she will turn into smoke, turn out to be a figment of my dreams. But she stays, under my lips, under my hips. Kissing Jade is magic: it is peaches so ripe the skin slides off, or butternut when butter melts into it, or chocolate on a rainy afternoon.

Her tongue, slithery as mango, wedges my teeth apart, toys with mine, then is gone again. Instinctively, my tongue forays after hers, deep into her sweet mouth.

Then she pulls away.

– Cool it, she laughs. I want it to last.

She pulls her cotton shirt over her head. Her breasts, freed, jelly bare and white under the moon. This is the moment of unveiling I have yearned for. I fall into a daze, transfixed as a chicken with its beak on a curved line chalked by a Zulu sangoma. I surface out of the daze into a feeling of fleeting panic, the panic I felt as a child in Durban faced with a choice of ice-cream. How to choose which nipple to lick first?

If this licking, this sucking of a girl is a sin, forgive me God but it is beautiful.

She tells me her lips are jealous of her nipples, so I kiss her lips again. Then, as the sky tints perlemoen pink, Jade unbuttons her shorts and slides my hand inside her lime-green panties. She tugs my white shorts down. My songololo is no longer the wormy, coy thing I have been ashamed of. He stands up, a charmed snake. I feel as if he will spit, but she whispers soothing things to calm him.

– You're beautiful, she purrs at him.

I have never thought of him as beautiful before. She tugs off her shorts and the lime-green panties and flicks them away and playfully wings her legs open and to. I gaze in wonder at her mossy kloof.

⁀

Afterwards, as I lie naked on the sand next to her, I wonder if it means we will be together forever.

– It was magic, Gecko, but I have a boyfriend. He's a bass guitarist in a band. I'm too old for you anyway, hey?

She kisses my forehead, buttons up her sex and tucks away her breasts.

In the glow of sunrise she drops her lime-green panties on my face and goes.

Fishermen wade out to haul a net onto the beach.

Gulls cry and scraps of coloured slang carry on the breeze, over the drum and lull of the waves.

# shebeen

I head for Jamaica Township again, this time in a taxi with Kala. He is coloured but has black chinas in the township and he goes to drink with them in a shebeen come Friday nights. Though I am seventeen, no longer the virgin boy of sixteen hooking on to Lars's Levi's, I still wish I had told someone where I was going. But who to tell? My father would kill me. Lars is lying low. Bach is long gone. Besides, it was a spur of the moment thing.

We, Zane and the Pniel boys, were playing cricket in the yard when Kala tuned me:

– Hey Gecko come along for a taxi ride to Jamaica, jus' for a shebeen beer.

– I dunno, Kala, I, I … I'm not so keen.

I did not tell him I am scared the police will catch me. Scared too of the rumour that they just drink sour, home-brewed beer in the shebeens and the sour beer makes a man do crazy things.

– Too scared to risk your soft white skin? Kala jibed.

So I had no choice. We caught the black mini-bus taxi just outside his school, a railway shed with a schoolyard stamped hard by the bare feet of kids skipping or playing soccer with a tennis ball or shuffling behind handmade wire jeeps. Wherever you go in South Africa you see such chock-full black taxis zooming along, but it is the first time I have been in one. My coins are handed forward from hand to hand to the driver and then the change comes back from hand to hand to me. The driver has his head way out of the window as he honks and whistles and hustles for another soul to sardine into his van.

Then we hit the teeth-jarring dirt roads of the township. The taxi weaves through endless rows of brick matchbox houses towards the shacks Matanga and the dancing girls taxi home to in the dark after another day of cooking Spur hamburgers and dustbinning and sweeping and petrol-jockeying and nodding *ja baas, ja baas* all day long in Paarl.

I jump out after Kala among the shacks. There is no bus stop, or sign to signal the shebeen. In the road a barber shaves a man's head with a razor blade. The hair falls in curling peels to the dust. A cobbler, sitting on a box, cuts a car tyre into the shape of a sole. Vendors sell slabs of raw, fly-peppered meat on newspaper. Hangdog dogs beg for handouts. Vivid oranges and tomatoes deck hawkers' stands.

Kala and I slink through back alleyways to keep out of sight of the wired-off police station up on the hill. The fortified white outpost reminds me of the Voortrekkers in their oxwagons surrounded by Zulu warriors. Instead of oxwagons, though, Casspirs shimmer in the sun.

An old man with thirsty-leather skin and a white beard squints at me from the junkyard seat of a motorcar he has propped against the wall of his shack. He cups a bowl of soured milk in his hands, thinking, perhaps, that this is a sad place to grow old, amid gutted motorcars, mangy dogs flicking pesky flies from their eyes, and bald chickens scratching among rags and bones and tins.

Rubbish swishswirls in the dustwind and collects in ditches or snags on barbed wire, like the random, painted graffiti on zinc walls:

they piss on us

MK is coming

one boer one bullet

My Minolta camera piedpipes kids out of alleyways. Soon there is a string of kids ragtagging at my heels. I shoot a spool of bobbing, shaven heads and gleaming teeth in front of the make-shift shops.

Inside the shebeen it is dark and cool and the fat shebeen queen gives Kala such a hug he almost drowns in the folds of her flowing dress.

Fortunately, she just shakes my hand and conjures a warm Lion beer for me.

Kala introduces me to his chinas. They all give their names. The only name that hooks in my mind is Angel, a tall boy with a pink scar on his forehead in the shape of a Nike wing. I wonder if it was a fall, or a fight, but do not dare ask.

The mute old men drink the sour beer in the murky corners, but Kala and his chinas drink bottled Lion and smoke ganja and tell stories of the tsotsi gangs, who knife you for a fiver if you stray onto their turf, and the way men sometimes vanish when they are detained by the police.

You may be detained for 90 days without a trial, they tell me. It is the law. Then, if you survive and they have got no case against you, they let you go. But if you do not bow your head as they give you back your clothes, and if your smile is too cocky, or your step too jaunty, they just pick you up again half a mile down the road and put you away for another 90 days. So it goes, if the police go by the book. If they don't go by the book, you are dead.

– So what do you think of the township? they quiz me.

– It sounds dangerous.

– It's okay if you visit with your camera, click and run, just like going to Safariland, chirps Angel.

They all laugh.

– But with the tsotsis and the police and all, it must be tricky to survive.

– Hey, you get by, Angel winks at me.

Again there is laughter and a clinking of beer bottles.

– You want to know how I picked up this? says Angel, fingering his scar.

I nod, but before Angel can tell his story, we hear a wild hooting and barking. We rush out of the shebeen to see a police van churn up dust. Squawking chickens shed feathers to the wind and dogs bolt. Doorways swallow blurred figures. Two policemen, one white, one black, jump out of the van, leaving the motor running. They batter against a tin door with their guns. When it does not open they kick it in.

They come out dragging a man whose heels groove the dirt. His cry is inhuman, the whine of a butcher's saw through bone. A comical sound to come out of a human mouth. A sound that, in a film, would make you laugh.

But there is no laughter. And no man runs to his rescue. We stand in the long dusk shadows, and watch.

They shove him into the back of the van and I hear the crack of his shins against the steel before he jack-knifes over. His face squashes up against the wire as the van roars into gear, kicks up spurs of dust, and guns out of sight.

Through the drifting dust, you can still hear his whining cries.

# maryjane

There is a haven in Paarl Boys' High, apart from the projection room and Mister Slater's classroom, and that is Miss Behr's room. Skinny Miss Behr is my guitar teacher and her jasmine scent is sweet after the sweat and urine of the changing rooms and the chalk dust of the classrooms.

Miss Behr has an Egon Schiele sketch of a naked girl on the wall, a memento of her time in Vienna, and wears a black grandpa vest with tortoise-shell buttons and a long black skirt that falls down to toenails painted in glossy peacock green. I wish to tunnel up Miss Behr's skirt and hide from yelling teachers and the fear of Baldhead Bosman's plum and the gnawing envy of Slimjan's writing.

Miss Behr found out long ago that I am no Dylan, that I have no inborn rhythm, but still she lets me come. I listlessly pluck the strings while we talk about books and things. She studied music at Rhodes University before going to Vienna for a year. She tells me about Vienna: the trams, the coffeeshops, the opera, the Danube. As she does so she gathers her long skirt in bunched folds until her bony knees stick out. She has pink notches on them. I hope her skirt will go higher, but she lets it fall when she sees me staring. She reaches for my hands and clasps them in hers.

– You know, you must go to the Grahamstown arts festival. It will be an oceanic experience for you.

I beg my mother and father to let me go, that it will be *oceanic*.

– Grahamstown is not on the sea, it is an hour inland from Port Alfred, my father jibes.

– But I want to study journalism and Rhodes is the place to go.

– Rhodes is so far, sighs my mother.

– I just want to see.

– Gecko, my boy, there are dangers there. Drugs and …

– Hippies, nods my father.

It is the first far journey I, big boy, am to make alone. My father forbids me to thumb a lift, so I sift through *The Cape Times* and find a lift with a medical student from UCT.

My father drives me to the rendezvous, the crossroads in Somerset West. My lift is an old painted hippie van brimful of students. The dogs go berserk in the back of the bakkie and my father nods itoldyouso.

It turns out the only medicine the medical student has studied is herbal.

– Ganja, kaya, grass, weed, boom, zol, doob, sweet maryjane, he intones as if he's a Tibetan priest reeling out a mantra.

The students drink Amstel beer.

– Castle Lager is too macho. Too white South African cock-swinging male.

So we go along the N2, Amstel in hand and Juluka at full volume. Though they offer me a drag of dagga, the weed is still too riddled with taboo for me. I remember Miss Hunter telling us dagga is one of the stops on the road downhill, before you end up joining the ANC. I remember Visoog Vorster giving a boy six cuts and then sending him packing for smoking dagga in the parking lot of the Protea Cinema. So I say *no thank you* and stay with the Amstel.

In half an hour you are over the Hottentots Holland Mountains, a journey that took days by oxwagon, and drop down into the Elgin and Grabouw apple orchards. Then, suddenly, you are in the yellow wheatlands of Caledon. The country dries out and you feel as if you are on the edge of a desert.

You pass through humdrum dorps: in each you see a police station, with the flag hanging listless in the heat and a mirage dancing on the hot tin roof.

You pass a one-star Royal or Grand hotel with an off-licence and a flypaper bar. Names that recall pioneering colonial days, when travellers stopped for more than petrol and a piss.

Coloured petroljockeys at the roadside BP and Shell garages lure you in with their flashy smiles.

Roadside cafés under Coca-Cola signs sell you take-away pies and Simba chips.

On the Port Elizabeth beachfront we park at a sixties roadhouse and watch seagulls flying into the wind without making headway.

Between Port Elizabeth and Grahamstown the countryside changes again. The scattered thorn and aloes and cycads, the clay huts and dongas and redearth anthills, give you the taste of Africa.

A donkey cart on the road, drifting through the haze.

Xhosa women in black turbans, carting firewood on their

heads. Jangling copper bangles that blink in the sun, dangling long, beaded pipes from their teeth. Young girls selling cactus figs or pineapples piled in pyramids.

Grahamstown is a snug, curled-up English hedgehog in the African veld. The Anglican cathedral at the foot of High Street dominates this town of church steeples and Victorian fronts. Beyond the cathedral I see the black township up on the hill.

Captain Malan taught me in History that Grahamstown was originally a fort on the far, frayed edge of the Cape Colony. Beyond Grahamstown and the Fish River was the dark unknown of the wild tribes.

⌒

In the High Street I hand over fifty rand, a cheap ride with the free Amstel and Juluka. A dry wind stirs up dust and paper behind me as I walk up High Street, past beggars and buskers and hawkers and milling students. After the uniform blues and greys of Paarl Boys' High it is bizarre to find myself among earringed throngs in sandals and rainbow kikois.

I see a play by Athol Fugard at The Box. The play is full of rage against apartheid and my heart beats fast at the racy dialogue. This Fugard character must be very brave. If he was at Paarl Boys' High, Visoog Vorster would cane him to a pulp.

At the end of the play those around me jump up to wave fists and toyi-toyi, thundering their feet to the pulsing cry of Nkululeku, freedom. Though I still feel self-conscious giving a black-power salute, I nevertheless wish my teachers at Paarl Boys' High could see me now: rooinek kaffirboetie on the barricades, jabbing my fist at imagined policemen and dogs and Casspirs.

There is a foreign film festival at the Odeon. In the cold gloom of the pre-war cinema I warm my hands with a packet of hot soggy chips from the Tamboowallah Café and fall in love with Isabelle Adjani's ebony hair on ivory skin.

A guitarman plucks Neil Young in the dusky dagga haze of a basement pub. Some folk find they hear the music better lying on the floor, or leaning their heads against the wall.

A girl with tumbling crow-black hair shares her glowing jay with me in a dark corner. In this smoky, bohemian, other world, the taboo fades. Before long I am well caned and things go all Dali on me.

I focus on a gecko on the roof and imagine it too is high, just breathing in the smoke. The girl draws my hand in under her skirt. I rub the rim of her vagina under cloth, till the damp seeps through.

Then she goes off to pee, and she walks upside down on the roof, skilfully, as if she has done it all her life. She leaves the glowing stompie of the jay in my hands. I am not sure if you stub it out or suck it till it goes out, so I suck it till it burns my fingers and I drop it to die in a hiss in the lees of a tumbler of red wine.

When she comes back down to me from her walkabout on the roof, I am far gone. Again my hand snakes into the dark between her knees. She has lost her panties and her shaven vagina feels smooth and warm as a newborn, bald rabbit.

Just then the world begins to reel. I plunge through blurred faces and jabbing shoulders and bared teeth, then I am on my knees barking the dog into piss.

I wade back through the haze to discover the girl is gone, rabbit and all.

Grahamstown station: I board the train bound for Cape Town. I yearn for the empty hours ahead, reading Steinbeck as the Karoo blurs by. The stone thirstland of telegraph poles and steel windmills.

First class is rich white and third class is non-white. That makes me second class, in a six-berth cabin. Apart from me, there is this guy in black leather from head to foot, bound for Maitland, that down-at-heel white suburb of Cape Town that picks up dust from the flats.

– Hey, my Maitland chinas call me Dippie, short for Dipstick.

He reels off a litany of his motorcars and motorcycles.

– I have an Alfa Spyder. Restored it all on my ace. But the most beautiful thing on earth is a Harley, tunes Dippie. So what's your game?

– I go to school. Paarl Boys' High.

I wonder if I will always have Paarl Boys' High pull down my head like a shotdown albatross.

– Hey, Paarl Boys'. I knew this chick in Paarl with big tits and the sweetest peach south of Bloemfontein, said Dippie.

I dare not ask Dippie if he has only been as far as Bloemfontein, or if there are even sweeter fruits beyond.

– Her old man jus' rots in the bloody station bar all day. One time he comes home drunk as a monkey and grabs his shotgun. The bastard shoots my backside fulla birdshot as I jump outa the window. I tell you, my china, peach can kill you.

We halt on some godforsaken, tumbleweed platform.

Dippie rabbits on about the lure of peach, of how you want it again and again.

– You know you gonna end up being shot at, or some bitch

shunts in with her bags and your freedom goes out the window, lock, stock and barrel. But still you go after it. Crazy, hey?

Through the window I see a sagging, unshaven old man saying goodbye to a young woman in red lipstick and spiked heels. Perhaps his daughter.

She folds a ten rand note into his jacket pocket. She kisses his cheek, smearing red lipstick on his white stubble. Then she tiptaps down the platform without glancing back.

When he comes into the cabin I see his jacket is threadbare and that one of the glass spheres from his glasses is gone. His breath reeks of booze. If the lipstick woman is his daughter, then she may be sending him south to another part of the family who will, I imagine, give him a shave and a meal and send him north again, another folded note in his pocket.

He sits on the bunk next to Dippie, who is subdued by the old man's hangdog face. Eventually Dippie thumps the old man on the back so hard his teeth drop out.

– Hey, Oupa. Howzabout I buy you a brandy, hey?

At that, Oupa perks up, pops his teeth in, and shuffles after Dippie to find the bar.

I pick up my book: *Of Mice and Men*. I am reading about Lennie dreaming of a rabbit farm, when a dogsick man stumbles into the cabin and lies down on the seat where Dippie and Oupa sat.

He tells me he is a sheep farmer from somewhere out Matjiesfontein way and has just had his appendix fished out.

– Do you want to see my scar?

– No. Thank you.

I fake a smile.

– Don't be shy, he tunes me.

He goes ahead and bares his stomach. A black-footed centipede slants down to his zip.

I smile feebly as I ride out waves of nausea.

– It hurts like hell. I should still be there by the hospital but I escaped, he laughs, the kind of *tee hee hee* laugh of one who outwits another in comics.

To prove he is suffering, he moans like a bleeding pig.

– Know why I ran away?

– The food?

– Hell no.

– The nurses?

– No. My sheep. They lost without me.

Dippie and Oupa come back to hit the sack and the sheep farmer uncovers his scar again. Not to disturb the farmer, they pull down the two bunks above my head. I am forced to abandon Steinbeck. I volunteer for the top bunk, to get as far away as I can from the dying man.

A steward comes round with fresh sheets. A chorus of grunts from below implies only moffies need sheets on a train, so I lie on the bare bunk and shut my eyes so I can fall asleep to the lulling rhythm of the wheels.

But it is tricky to drift off. Dippie on the bunk below me degobs his throat between drags on his Gunston fag. Oupa weeps and his teeth rattle in a glass on the sink. Not to be outdone, the sheep farmer whines every now and then.

Then Oupa kicks off his shoes and I gasp for air at the tilted window.

The train whistles through a dorp of jackal-eye windows and my romantic illusions of travelling by train blow out into the cold, black Karoo with Dippie's Gunston smoke.

# warrior

My school days are over. I have time to explore Cape Town during the long Christmas holidays.

WHITES ONLY signs mark benches and beaches. Mandela is in his cell on Robben Island, across the seagull bay. But apartheid is fraying at the edges. In the streets of Cape Town you sometimes see a black guy with a white girl or a black girl with a white guy.

And things change in other ways.

French and German girls drop their bikini tops on the beach at Clifton and Llandudno to bare perky breasts to the sun. Sometimes, down a back street someone will peel out of the shadows, like a conscience, and offer you some grass:

– Swazi, pure and cheap.

Short summer skirts flutter by and flowergirls and fruitsellers gaily call their wares but I drag my feet through the swirl of life and colour. My long and bitter days at Paarl Boys' High are through and I ought to feel that carefree summer mood flow through my blood:

Languid days on the farm.

The deep dark cool of the dam.

Cricket under the pines.

Tennis on the sand court.

Beer mugs of Oros and ice.

(Once a tadpole came through the pipes from the dam and my mother found it frozen in a block of ice in her g & t.)

Reading in my room by candle. Moth wings burning in a spit of flame.

Instead, a shadow hangs over me and clogs the air, for I have my call-up. I am to report to the infantry camp in Oudtshoorn in a fortnight. I had hoped I might be sent to the navy base at Saldanha where the Berg River runs into the sea. There I would still feel umbilically joined to the valley and the vineyards through the river. But no, I am to go over the mountains to Oudtshoorn in the Karoo, where the gawky ostriches scratch for stones in the dust.

Tinsel and fake snow in the shops. Parcel-burdened shoppers look the other way when tattered streetkids tug at their clothes. It is crazy to think of Santa and his reindeer while the sun melts the tar.

I wish I was free to skip the country on a Danish passport as Lars did. It is either the army or jail for me, and after all Lars's stories of torture and flying from high windows, I am shit scared of jail.

A dry berg wind breathes down from Lion's Head and stirs up dust and paper and the distant sound of chanting. And, as in a dream, the tapdancer in St George's Street slows his rhythm and the flowersellers hold out their proteas in silence.

The chanting filters down from somewhere over the BoKaap until a human river flows down Wale Street and into the city and overflows onto the pavements of Adderley Street. At the head of the tide, fists wave and ululating women ripple their shoulders and swing their hips at the police.

The riot police lean against their yellow vans in the sun. They lovingly pat their guns, grind cigarette stubs under black boots. Their dogs whimper, begging to be loosed.

The human river dams against the wall of police and vans and dogs. Women whistle and jive. Men stab their fists into the sky. Thousands of wardancing feet slam into the tar.

– Amandla amandla amandla, cry the fists.

A paternal voice booms over the chanting and the whistles and stomping:

– This is an unlawful gathering. You must all go home in peace …

His voice is drowned in crowing laughter.

Eyes glow with the rush of baiting the regime – on streets the marchers swept or bussed to work on.

My mind switches into slow motion as a head a few inches away from mine snaps back.

And then, only, do I hear the pop of rubber bullets and the cries like blades scything through the air.

I plunge through a mist of teargas and coldfear eyes. I feel pain sear through my head.

*I see, as in the dark of a cinema, marchers running like a herd of wildebeest towards the bank of a raging river. Looking back, they see Land Rovers coming after them. Bushmen trackers perch on the roofs and policemen gaze down the barrels of their guns. The hunted plunge into the river. Crocodiles and sharks glide in among the frenzy.*

*Then I'm standing on the bank of the blood-suffused river. I turn to see Visoog Vorster and Maljan and the De Beer brothers coming after me. On the far bank Lucky Strike beckons to me. I dive in among the crocodiles and sharks to be jawed to death. But the water falls away, as if sucked down a plughole.*

*I corkscrew down and down and down until a wind whisks me up and I see, again, our house in Natal far below. I see the old jacaranda and Tomtom at the backyard wire and Beauty jellying* with laughter as she pegs up the washing and Jonas giggling as he rolls his Boxer tobacco.

Lucky Strike jigs outside the kitchen door with Dingaan and Dingo, calling:

– Fly fly fly, young baas.

I fly as I have never flown before, over the rolling hills of Zululand and over the Drakensberg mountains.

Across the Karoo, a scattering of sheep and koppies and windmills.

Across the Hex River valley and over the Du Toitskloof mountains.

Until I see our white, gabled house in the shadow of the Simonsberg: Zane and Langtand and Kala and Flip van Staden playing cricket under the pines, and Lars swinging on the gate across the road.

I wish they would look up, but only Flip tilts his dead-fish stare at the sky as I fly by.

⁓

I come to under stiff white sheets to see my mother's black mascara tears and my father gaunt and drawn.

– Thank you Jesus, my mother mutters.

– You ran into a lamppost. You had your mother and me scared to death, my father says.

Biko dead and Mandela in jail for their beliefs. Me, I run shit-scared blind, headlong into a lamppost. So much for the warrior.

# a dry white season

A parcel comes for me. The outer manila envelope has been ripped and taped up again with masking tape by the customsmen who check for contraband: Cuban cigars, dagga, *Playboy*, Communist books. Fortunately the paper underneath bears a Christmas motif of angels. They are, after all, Christian. The lady at the post office says: Sorry hey, it is just routine. I see the stamps of the Danish queen. It is the banned book I have asked Lars to send, *A Dry White Season*. If the police catch you with it you are for the high jump. I have just turned eighteen, which means I will no longer be beaten by the police as Spud was after stealing cigarettes. I will be sent to jail with hardened men, who have raped and stabbed.

I cycle up to the reservoir, hide my bicycle in the peach orchards and climb the curving wall. I jump down to the dusty, weedy floor. Lizards scurry into cracks in the wall as I land. Now I am alone. Just pigeons in the bluegums eye me. I tear through the manila paper and slide out the Christmas-papered book. *A Dry White Season*, by André Brink. I am so aware of holding a forbidden, contraband thing in my hands, I half expect the police dogs to sniff it out and the police to vault the walls. My heart still aflurry, I open the book to discover a note from Lars. *Enjoy. Skip the foreword, it gives the ending away. Love, Lars.* A pity there is no cloak-and-dagger drama in his words. No tip on hiding the book, burning the evidence. Perhaps he has lived too long in Europe, too long beyond the reach of fear.

I read the poem in the front of the book, by Mongane Wally Serote. It goes: *It is a dry white season.* I look up at the green gums brushing the blue sky and wonder how the world can ever be white. In Serote's white world, a world bled of colour, the dry leaves dive. They do not bleed, just the trees feel pain. My mother would nod and sigh at the words, but to me it is puzzling. This is the first time I have ever read the words of a black man. I have heard the words of black men sung, but never seen their words on paper. All the signs, all the newspapers, all the books I have ever read were written by white men.

I hide the photo of the woman with the Coca-Cola bottle in her, in the book. In for a penny in for pound.

⌒

I rescue a Cape eagle owl from being stoned by a band of coloured boys. I call the owl Camus and feed him raw meat rolled in the rabbit fur I brush out of my angora rabbit. My father brings home birds that have been caught in traps in the vineyards. One day I find Camus on the floor, his feet in the air.

# pink flowers

In the Blue Note Café in Cape Town I write a postcard to Lars in Copenhagen while the softjazz *Art of Tea* plays on the jukebox. *Love is monkey see and monkey do*, go the words. As I write, I imagine Lars's life as a blend of Jim Jarmusch and Neil Young and Steely Dan and endless filter coffees.

Just a few days of freedom to go, I write, then I head out for Oudtshoorn. I am scared of what they will do to me when I tell them I will not carry a gun. What do they do? Do they throw you in the DB cells? Do they hound you, wear you down, till you beg to be given a gun?

When the jukebox dies I look up to see a blonde girl reading alone. She is reading *Out of Africa*. Her cappuccino is empty and has left foamy rings against the white china to reveal that she sipped it slowly. How could I not have sensed her being there?

With my heart in my mouth, I say:

– It's a beautiful book, don't you find?

She tips it to glance at the cover.

– I read it in school in Danish and thought it might be fun to read out here, you know, in Africa.

– You're Danish?

– Ya.

– I'm just writing to a friend in Copenhagen. He's like a brother to me. We lived across the road, not in Copenhagen but here. Well, not actually here in Cape Town but out there on a farm, over the Simonsberg. Anyway, we are like brothers.

– Have you ever been to Copenhagen?

–Me? God no. I haven't been anywhere. I mean I've been hunting in Botswana. Not that I'm a hunter or anything. I've never been overseas. I haven't even been to Robben Island.

It is one of my father's jokes, but it falls flat.

London, Copenhagen: it's all a hazy dream to me.

– Lars, my friend, sent me a postcard of the harbour in Copenhagen with all the old boats and pastel houses and cafés.

– They call it Nyhavn. Hans Christian Andersen lived there, did you know? I used to go down there after school to eat snails by the harbour.

She laughs at my screwed-up face. Her laughter is a scattering of beads.

– Not the snails you're thinking of, but pastry snails that wind round and round and taste *mmmm*.

– Lars, he goes down to the harbour sometimes. Maybe someday he and I will drink a Carlsberg there and look for mermaids and I will say: Hey, you know I once met a Danish girl in Cape Town reading *Out of Africa*, which Karen Blixen wrote in Denmark, while I was writing to you in Copenhagen.

– And not just a Danish girl, but a girl from Copenhagen.

– Bizarre isn't it?

I am glad I used the word bizarre. It sounds philosophical.

– Hey, are you free at all? Just for the afternoon, maybe. We could go to the gardens and get an ice-cream or something?

– Sure, why not? But call me Zelda.

My heart is a flotilla of butterfly wings.

An old bag lady who carries her world in a rusty trolley sells us a bag of nuts to feed the grey squirrels in the gardens. They are so tame they brush against your fingers before darting away.

– The squirrels in Denmark are red, Zelda tells me.

We get ice-cream and Zelda heads for a patch of lawn where a sign warns: KEEP OFF THE GRASS. She flops onto the grass and laughs her scattered-bead laugh at me when I stall.

– It's because everyone obeys the signs that no one is free in this country, she says.

So I join her on the grass but I feel self-conscious, as if all the strollers and hobos are looking skew at us. She hitches up her tartan dress, like a schoolgirl wanting to skip a rope, and bares her legs to the sun. She tells me she is staying with her father who is some big shot in the Danish consulate and has a larney flat in Hout Bay over the mountain. She hardly ever sees him.

– Shall we picnic on the beach at Hout Bay? go her pink ice-creamed lips.

– Sure, why not?

All deadpan. But, inside, there is a flurry of butterfly wings again.

We pick up two bottles of red wine, a stinking wedge of Brie, a long baguette, and jump on a bus that winds around the peninsula.

Past the lighthouse at Geen Point.

Past the Hard Rock Café on Beach Road, where The Mamas and The Papas are forever *California Dreamin'* as the seagulls bob and dip in the wind.

I am on cloud nine as I look at the sunlight on her straw-blonde hair. I have never felt so alive and all my senses are on edge. I am aware of Zelda's smell.

– Loulou, she tells me.

The late afternoon sun dances on the water through the Camps Bay palms. I was once tumbled by a wave in Camps Bay when we first came to the Cape. Sand filled my mouth and salt-water stung my eyes and I didn't know where the sky was. My father fished me out.

Another way to die in the Cape.

My legs sweat against the red vinyl seat where they jut out of my khaki bermudas. To get my skin off the seat I rest my knees against the back of the seat in front, just as I did all those years on the bus to Paarl. Zelda copies me. I lean against her to catch a glimpse of the rocks down at Llandudno and the wine bottles in my rucksack clink cheerfully.

We hop off the bus in Hout Bay where the road winds down from Chapman's Peak. The beach curves from the road to the harbour, where fish-laden trawlers chug in. Once, with my mother and father, we bought fresh snoek off the boats and watched the green-dungareed fishermen gut the fish so their stringy insides spilt into the dusk. Then the fishermen flung the oozy spill into the harbour for the gulls and the sharks.

Zelda and I find a bench between the car park and the sea. The car park is deserted but for two lovers in an orange VW Beetle with a surfboard on the roof. Once again I feel self-conscious, as I did on the grass, for the Beetle lovers create a mood.

I dig out the Kenyan kikoi Lars sent me from Nairobi, on his way to Copenhagen. I fold it out on the sand as a picnic cloth and find stones to keep the corners from peeling up in the breeze. As we have no corkscrew I bang the cork down into the bottle.

The sea is bathed in the orange glow of dusk. Time stands still like those afternoons in Natal when the air was luminous and tinged with green after a thunderstorm and the world was on the verge of something profound. I feel a longing to kiss Zelda deeply and pray to my lonely God, and to the Bushman-god moon over Noordhoek, and to Venus born out sea foam, that Zelda will fall for me.

I comb my fingers through her hair and she tilts her head towards me. I kiss her forehead and her eyes, edging ever closer to her until my lips touch hers.

A bakkie of yahooing boys kicks up the dust of the parking bay. They wolfwhistle at us and at the Beetle lovers. A beer can bounces off the roof of the Beetle. Then the bakkie goes. The Beetle lovers, rattled by the clanging can, head for the harbour lights.

Alone on the beach, our lips touch again. We kiss deeply, the ebb and flow of the waves a soundtrack to the surge and lull of lust. Her mouth tastes of girl and wine. Loulou mingles with the smell of mist off the sea. My fingers follow the nodes of her spine down to the line of her panties, and rub her there in a slow pivot. She reaches for my other hand, still on the wine bottle. The bottle tips and wine colours the kikoi red.

Zelda holds my hand to her breasts. Through the fabric under my palm I feel her nipples go hard. I hardly dare breathe, fearing the spell will break.

– You like my hills? Zelda teases.

– Zelda, I want to stay among your hills for always.

Zelda falls back on the kikoi, her hair in the sand. She wiggles her hips to free her dress and lift it over her head. The flicker of distant headlamps plays on her skin. I want to let her breasts fill my mind as they fill my mouth, but guilt and the fear of cruising beerboys linger like stray dogs in the shadows just beyond firelight.

When a cold wind blows in off the sea, we go up to her house. The house is modern with French doors to the balcony. On the glass coffee-table lie French books of photographs of nude women against rocks and driftwood. I peek at the photographs while Zelda makes filter coffee in a coffee machine. I think of my folks' untaboo books: Roberts's book of birds and J.L.B. Smith's book of fish. I think of the way that we always drink Van Riebeeck instant coffee on the farm. A teaspoon flippantly tipped in, instead of this slow seeping through paper, this gurgling and spitting, that goes into making good coffee.

Zelda dims the light and we kiss on the sofa between sips of coffee. When I want her breasts again, she leads me up to her room. She undresses in front of me. I love the fleeting moment when her dress hoods her head, turns her into a headless Greek sculpture, skin toned stone white under the glaring bulb. And though I had her nipples in my mouth on the beach, I stare in wonder at the floating pink flowers.

Then she dives under the blue cover.

– Aren't you coming in? she teases as her face surfaces.

An echo of my mother calling me to jump into the cold sea in Gordon's Bay. It's fine once you're in, is my mother's line. I switch off the light to undress, but you can still see by the moon. I am glad she left her panties on so that I do not have to stand there stark naked in the moonshine.

Again I suck her nipples. Her hands go all over me, as if she is colouring me in recklessly.

Then, instead of staying cool and letting my tongue drift down to her vagina, I tell her I have to go away to the army. Desolation overcomes me. She holds my head to her breast until her skin is wet with my snot and tears. It changes the mood and we end up just holding. We promise each other to meet again one day in Cape Town or Copenhagen and that it will be beautiful again.

# dust time

Blood on the tar. A vulture drops out of the blue. The bald bird lands on the edge of the hot tar and flaps and jerks towards the dead sheep. The bird glances up and down the road for the death machines that beat along the tar from out of sight to hell and gone. It darts its pink neck into the raw and then flicks its blooded scalp up again.

Still no motorcars. Only the parched land and the road scarring through it and a steel windmill that sucks up water from under the bone-dry earth and a farmhouse: a distant blot on the veld like a tick on a drought-ravaged ox.

I stand in the shaft of shade of a road sign that stands out stark as a totem against the blue sky. The vulture blinks a beady eye at me.

A truck comes into view. The vulture hobbles off. I step out of the shade to cock my thumb. The truck, bound for the killing yard with a cargo of deathrow sheep, jars to a halt.

Sheep and I jam together on the back, under the flaming sun. The trucker chucks me a can of lukewarm Lion.

Barrydale. Ladismith. Calitzdorp. Further and further away from the valley of Groot Drakenstein, where the Simonsberg drinks the blood-orange sunset, and fruit-laden tractors clang down the bluegum avenue. Ever deeper into the arid, sheep-piss Karoo.

⁓

I arrive at the barbed gates. This side of the wire: the garden gnomes and swings and swimming pools of the free. Beyond: the dust drillyard and brick barracks of my fears. I am, again, the schoolboy on the bus walking towards Spook and his crocodile teeth. The earth tilts. I reel under the wilting orange, white and blue flag.

– Hey you. You lost or something? chirps a soldier in the shadow of a tall box. The kind of box you see in postcards of London with the guards in red jackets and black bearfur busbees.

From the box I can just make out the sound of cricket on a radio. As my freedom goes, other folk in South Africa play cricket or surf or dive into cool water.

– No, I am not lost. I got my call-up.

– Well, come through. The colonel is waiting for you with koeksisters and a cup of tea.

I smile faintly at his bitter joke and walk into the camp with my yellow scubabag biting into my shoulder. As I reach the drillyard, milling, hippie-haired boys from Cape Town are herded into rows. A stumpy, hairy-armed man yells at me from the gaping hole under his walrus moustache:

– Hey you standing there like a blerrie fool.

– Me?

– Ja you. Fall in with the other baboons.

I join the ranks of the other dazed boys and see my fear in their eyes.

– I'll turn you from a tribe of baboons into a band of men

hool kill or be killed for Sowefrika. I gonna be on your bek day and night.

I put up my hand, as if I am still in Paarl Boys' High, asking Baldhead Bosman a biology question.

– Sir, if you don't mind I'd rather not shoot a gun.

I stop short of saying that, if it is all the same to everyone, I'd also rather not be shot.

All the rigours of crawling through the Angolan bundu in search of Cubans have not equipped the man for such betrayal from his own ranks. His fiery eyes twitch. I have the feeling that he would rip my head off with his bare hands if we were out in the bush. The other recruits shuffle their feet in the dust, as if they are about to witness a hanging.

– Boy, if you ever call me sir again, I keel you dead. You call me sarmajoor. You hear?

– Yes sir sarmajoor, I say.

Venom glints in his eyes. He makes me stand alone in the middle of the sun. Through the cursing of the corporals, who fuss around the sergeant major like pilot fish around a shark, I make out the distant jingle of a lollyboy's bell beyond the barbed wire. In the distance, stone mountains fall away in paling shades of grey.

Then we are all jackbooted to the barber to be shaved. I have to wait until the others emerge like a colony of skinhead Krishnas, then the sarmajoor makes me sweep all the hair into a corner before it is my turn. My hair feathers to the floor. I almost cry when the barber winks at me. On his radio Cat Stevens sings: *oh baby, baby it's a wild world, it's hard to get by just upon a smile, girl.*

I stand in my underpants in a warehouse as a man called Staff takes my yellow scubabag with my civvy clothes inside, tags it, and trades it for a brown overall, boots and tin hat. My bag is tossed onto a heap that reminds me of photographed pyramids of gutted Jewish suitcases on railway platforms.

I do not sleep in the long cement barracks but alone in an empty DB cell as if I have yellow fever. I rub my shaven head as I stare at the shadow of the bars cast by the moon. A soldierboy before me has scratched the word *Marie* into the wall. I wonder if his Marie waited the two years for him and if they got married, maybe live on a farm somewhere with dogs and kids and a bakkie.

☞

The days are an endless barrage of barked commands and boots hammering into the earth. You breathe and taste dust. Grains of dust scrape under your eyelids and grind between your teeth. While others do gun drill, I scrub out the toilets, pick up cigarette stubs flicked through the windows of the officers' canteen, or march with bricks in my hands instead of a gun.

☞

Today, the sarmajoor ordered me to march past a row of chairs and salute each chair as if it were an officer. It is a change from toilet scrubbing and stub collecting, but after two hours of saluting unfeeling chairs under the sun, I begin chancing it and salute every other chair. The chairs do not mind and I fall into the rhythm:

Officer chair coming up: turn my head and touch the brim of my beret.

NCO chair coming up: point thumbs down at boots.

Officer chair coming up: turn head and touch brim of beret.

NCO chair: Thumbs down.

Officer chair: Salute.

So it goes.

Then comes the sound that makes my heart skip a beat: the *vroom vroom* of the sarmajoor's Suzuki. Damn. I flamboyantly salute the next chair, even though it is NCO, but the vulture-eyed sarmajoor has seen my gyppoing.

Still on his Suzuki, over the rumble of the motor, he spits out his words:

– Are you crazy in the head or what?

I halt, stamping my feet down into the dust in the hope he will forgive me if I pull off a tidy halt.

The Suzuki motor dies. Behind him, Corporal Boyd runs up.

The sarmajoor's face is two inches from mine.

– I told you to salute every blerrie chair.

– But sir, I mean sarmajoor, I thought the bentwood chairs might be corporals, and I knew you would not think it right if I saluted them.

Again the beetroot red floods his face and his eyelids flip up and down.

Boyd offers him his water bottle, but the sarmajoor smacks it out of his hands. The water is blotted up so fast, it is as if it falls through the earth.

– Corporal, march this rooinek communist to the DB.

In his rage the sarmajoor forgets that I, rooinek communist, sleep in the DB cells anyway, so it is hardly a punishment to be locked up in there with Marie on the wall.

Today it is my job to water the flowerbeds in front of the HQ. Every now and again the sarmajoor abandons the other platoons to their neverending gun drill and rides over to HQ on his Suzuki to check up on me.

I am watering the colonel's red and yellow cannas, the only patch of colour besides the oranje blanje blou in this Karoo outpost, when I hear the growl of the Suzuki again. Just as he Suzukies up to me, the water in my hosepipe peters out. The tap is far away, around the corner. Perhaps someone turned it off, or parked a jeep on the pipe, pinching it shut. I shake out the last sad drops over the thirsty earth while the sarmajoor just shakes his head at this final proof of my worth to the South African Army. I will not shoot a gun at the enemy and I cannot even handle a hosepipe for southafricadearland.

My bed in the DB cell has steel springs that twang and bend. The mattress sags incurably, but the sarmajoor expects it to be as flat as a runover rabbit for inspection each morning.

I prop the bed up with wooden pegs squeezed between the mattress and the springs, some sideways and some straight up. I iron the sheets and bite their edges until all is flat and square. I scrub the floor and iron my browns until they hang stiff in the steel cupboard. I rub my boots with Kiwi and spit until they glint. The spit is a trick of my father's from his boarding-school days.

I lie down under the bed on the cold cement to sleep, hoping to dream of Zelda.

Instead images float up from the dark pool of my mind:

The sheep's head in the Zulu firepot.

The bones of Box down the dry well.

The crab cracking against the tar.

And Bulldog's crazed eyes.

At sunrise Corporal Boyd bangs on the door.

– Staaaaaaaaaaaaaaaanop, he yells.

I jump to my feet and stand stiff as the sarmajoor comes in. He runs his finger along the top of the steel cupboard but does not find any dust there. Then he gazes up at the light bulb to see if perhaps a smudge of subversive dirt lurks there. He bears a smug grin as if he has caught out many a green recruit in this way before. To finger the light bulb for evidence, he steps onto the bed. Pegs shoot out in every direction. The sarmajoor lunges for the hanging bulb, as you would reach for the leather noose dangling from a hand rail in a tilting bus. The bulb pops in his hands but the cable holds his bulk as he swings out. Then it rips out of the roof and he falls to the cement floor.

He lies there among shards of broken glass and scattered pegs and bleeding hands. He has survived Russian Migs and Cuban soldiers and all the hazards of bush war to be undone by a bed.

From the floor he barks at me:

– Vandag is opfok dag.

The sarmajoor stands in the shade of a plane tree while he keeps an eye on the opfok drill: me marching on the double, jigging up and down as if the strings of a puppeteer in the sky tug at my knees. But above there is no puppeteer or god, only swifts dipping and gliding in the glare. Beads of sweat pool with the tears in my eyes, so that the sarmajoor is just a hazy form. When I blink away the film of bitter water, I see him clearly, for a while. Thumbs hooked through his belt loops. Sun glinting off his 32

Battalion buffalohead belt. Then the outlines smudge again.

And whenever the puppet strings go slack and I tumble to the hot earth and bark the dog, Corporal Boyd splashes water in my face to revive me. Then my knees jerk up again to the beat of Boyd's relentless voice:

– Lik lak lik lak lik lak laaaaai lik lak lik lak lik lak laaaaaaaaai.

On and on and on until the sky tilts again. A doctor stands there too, in the planetree shade, and sometimes comes over with the sarmajoor to see if I am truly fainting or just acting half-dead. He looks ashamed of his part in it and I want to tell him I understand but no words come out. The sarmajoor smirks at the sight of a communist gasping like a gaffed fish.

In the end, when I spit blood, the doctor says they will kill me if this goes on.

– Hou op, the sarmajoor orders Boyd.

A *lik* catches in Boyd's gullet.

The sarmajoor stalks away across the drillyard with Boyd at his heels.

# nirvana

I drop to the other side of the wire and freeze, waiting for the night to flare and a bullet to bite. But the darkness does not stir, so I cross the tar. I find a lumberjack shirt pegged on a line. I trade the overalls for the shirt, which comes down to my knees. Leaving my army duds hanging on the line like a shed skin, I run along the tarred, lamplit streets of Oudtshoorn, with just my passport in a pocket and my yearning for freedom.

In army tackies the colour of shit and a lumberjack shirt as long as a dress, I head south, towards Wilderness and the sea. I hope the sarmajoor will look for me on the westbound Calitzdorp road to Cape Town. I run hard until the road begins to slant up into the Outeniqua Mountains. At the flicker of headlamps I drop into a ditch like a hunted jackal. I wait until the red eyes of the motorcar fade before I begin to run again.

All fagged out, I creep into a stormwater culvert and lay my head on the dry river sand. I fall into a fitful sleep, dreaming of the sarmajoor and Boyd coming after me in a tank and of stray ostriches reaching their long, snaky necks deep into the culvert to peck my eyes out.

The morning lies cold on my face and my heart beats into the sand as a lone motorcar whines up the mountain pass. In the daylight I cannot believe I am a deserter to be hunted down like a dog, but jumping the wire I can never undo, never rewind.

I hear another motorcar in the distance and peek out to see a yellow bakkie pulling into the curves. I stay down, for there is just a chance it could be the police or the army. I am not sure who comes to look for you if you run away from the army but I imagine the rabid sarmajoor at the wheel, baying for blood.

The yellow bakkie goes by with a black man on the back, and dogs barking madly at the wind. It reminds me of my father driving Nero and Fango up to the dam in the evenings. By running away I have cut myself off from my mother and my father and Zane and the valley. I want to cry, but I spy a white VW Beetle with surfboards on the roof. I instinctively jump out of the culvert and wave, as if it might be Lars come to rescue me.

The Beetle chugs to a halt. Behind the wheel is a guy with straggling surfblond hair and those sunglasses with bits of leather on the sides, like the blinkers on a donkey. He checks out my lumberjack dress and army tackies.

– Cool gear. Where ya heading? he tunes.

– As far as you go.

He, still eyeing me over:

– I'm heading for Nahoon, East London. Cool surf. Maybe you heard of it?

– Sorry.

He nods as if it confirms some theory of his. I wonder if I will be stranded forever in the desert because I am not tuned into the surfing scene.

– Jump in, he says.

A last glance down the windy road at the distant haze that is Oudtshoorn, then I jump in.

– By the way, I'm Peejay.

– I'm Gecko.

– Far out, he laughs.

The Beetle is jam-packed with bags and books and a guitar. I have to put my feet up on a black box, an amp or something, so that I look at the road through my knees. There is no place to duck out of sight. I am as exposed as a dog on the beach.

– So, where'd you pick up the army tackies?

– Greenmarket Square, I fib.

– Check out this theory: you find a jack half-naked in the desert with army tackies on his feet and his hair shaven like a fucking sheep, chances are you've found a deserter. Just chuck the shoes out the window before we hit civilisation.

So I chuck the tackies and watch them dance on the tar in the rearview mirror. Then I put on some old sandals he gives me.

My eyelids droop.

☞

I dream a black man is waving at me. He is so close I can see the pores in his skin. He flashes friendly teeth at me.

Then I cotton on: he is not waving, but wiping. I am not dreaming. Framed between the sandals with my sore feet inside, he is wiping the windshield free of grasshopper and butterfly flecks. We have stopped at a garage.

I look around for Peejay. There he is. He has dropped his head into a deep icebox. His jeans pull taut across his ass so that I make out strawberry-patterned boxers through a frayed rent. How Visoog Vorster would have loved to swing his cane down on that sassy ass. Peejay comes over with two cans of Coca-Cola and smiles to see me awake.

– Hey, sexy, wanna Coke?

He is still amused by my running wild in the desert in my lumberjack dress. I giggle, but then recall that I am a deserter.

Peejay senses my fear.

– Be cool, dude. We've made good time. Besides, they'll look south.

My legs hurt from the opfok drill and the run up into the mountains. I get out of the crammed Beetle to free my legs and keel over onto the oil-dappled cement. Peejay and the petroljockey pick me up and sit me on the running board.

The petroljockey's pink-skin boss squints at us and picks his teeth in front of his pin-ups. I sit half in shade and half in the burning sun and hold the cold Coca-Cola can against my forehead. It is so still without the gunshots and barked commands: just the now-and-then drone of motorcars, and the creak of a windmill. I almost dare to feel free but the pigman's squint rattles me.

Peejay tips the petroljockey.

– Go well, calls the petroljockey after us.

On the way out of town, we pick up soggy chips and chicken pies at a café. There is a blue-painted bar across the street, the only colour in the drab, dry town. A faded red sign reads: Oasis Bar and Grill. The sun has peeled her blue dress and kissed the gloss off her red sign.

Paul Simon sings *Gumboots* and the sun dances on the VW hood.

– We'll be in Jay Bay by noon, says Peejay, drumming his fingers against the wheel. They must have buggered you around in Oudtshoorn, hey?

– Yesterday they drilled me so long and hard I had blood in my mouth.

– I heard they give you a baby monkey or cat or something and you feed it and all until it's attached to you and then you have to kill it with your bare hands.

– I never had to kill a monkey.

– Dude, I tell you, when they come for me I'm gonna go down under. Just ass around on the Reef, you know.

– Australia sounds good to me. You would still have the sun and the blue skies and the sea.

– And the girls, tunes Peejay.

– And the girls, I echo, wondering if Zelda dreams of me.

We coast into Jay Bay under a burning, zenith sun. Two girls in bikini tops and frayed denim skirts balance sixpacks of beer on their heads, the way Xhosa women on country roads carry suitcases or firewood. Peejay whistles at the girls and they laugh.

– This is Jay Bay, surfers' nirvana. Kiffest waves on the planet, Peejay tells me.

Peejay parks on the fringe of the beach, where the grass gives way to the sand. Surfers languidly wax boards with Mr Zog's Sexwax and dangle rubber Reef arms from their hips, like penguin wings. Their movements are so liquid after the jerky marching of soldiers across the dust plains. Peejay clasps hands with old chinas who flick tangled hair out of their eyes.

I stand there, forgotten, shaven and uncool. I feel whittled down by the army.

After some time, I kick off Peejay's sandals and wander alone down to the sea. I dig my toes into the cold wet sand and feel the backwash tug at my heels and the sun burn my skin. I breathe in the salt mist and think of Hout Bay and Groot Drakenstein. I cry for the lost magic of Zelda's breasts and for my mother's smell.

A hand rubs my shaven head. It is Peejay and a dragon spitting flames across his Billabong surfboard.

– Hey, dude. Those army fuckers can't swim. If they come after you, you just dive in and drift until some Brazilian baby with big coconuts tugs you out of the sea and gives you the kiss of life.

He rubs my head again and his smile blurs through my tears. Then he runs and dives, dipping his surfboard under the waves and surfacing beyond. He paddles out with deep, swift strokes. When he is through the breakers he turns to wave at me. I wave back, thinking he is so cool the way he duckdives through the waves.

I too want to be out there, beyond the reach of the sarmajoor. I drop the lumberjack shirt onto dry sand and wade out. I dive through a wave and then freestyle out to the surfers. Seagulls skim along the edge of the waves as swiftly as a spinner's hand across the weave. The salt stings my eyes.

The surfers in their black sealskins float on the water and wait solemnly for the high waves after the lull. Bobbing monks waiting for illumination. Waiting until, by some accident of tide and sand, the big wave with the long slow break is formed. Then the sudden spin and paddle until the world drops away and they stand to glide.

Sometimes I duck to avoid being cut by a surfboard fin and I peer down into the deep shadowy blue for the fin I most fear: a shark's.

We camp in the lee of the motorcars just as the Voortrekkers did in the shelter of oxwagons in the old days. We sit around a fire drinking cans of Castle while boerewors sizzles over the flame. The surfers all have stories to tell of wild surf in Durban and Nahoon. Some have been overseas to surf Uluwatu and Oahu. But still, they say, Jay Bay is the ultimate long ride.

No one thinks to ask me about the army and perhaps that is a good thing for there is nothing cool about saluting chairs and gathering cigarette stubs. The telling of it would sour the chill vibe. Swirling the bitter beer in my mouth, I think of how Karoo dust has been my beach sand and the canvas browns my Gotcha gear. Peejay has given me a pair of threadbare cords, patched at the knees, and they feel light and cottony on my skin after the heavy browns.

The denim girls from earlier are there, by the fire, and wear twin yellow jerseys. A vivid yellow to be tasted in your mouth. So alluring after the shit-brown overalls and hay-brown dust.

Mesmerised, I watch one of the yellow girls roll a jay. Her fingers pinch and rub and scatter tobacco and grass into the paper furrow. Then she licks the paper, rolls it, and twists one end.

Again I think of Zelda and the twisting of the paper cone filled with peanuts to feed the squirrels. How cool she was to lift her dress on the grass for the sun and my eyes to linger on her bare skin.

The jay flares and then glows like a spark that jumped the fire. After a while the girl gets careless about closing her legs and the firelight flickers in the hollow below the lip of her skirt.

The other yellow girl sucks the jay so that it glows again and then lets it drift away into other hands. She stares so long and deeply into the fire that I wonder what she sees. As a child I always made out animals in the fire: flamingos and cobras. I try to see them again but all I see is blue-tinged orange.

As the fire teases my sandalled toes, I wonder if my untravelled paths are still mapped out in the stars, or if I have defied destiny by jumping the wire. Am I now heading down unmapped roads to a hazy place of exile, beyond the horizon, beyond destiny?

All the familiar landmarks have gone:

The sighing stone pines.

The Dutch house under the bluegum.

The old palm. Undutch.

The lemon tree, a ladder to the pumpkin roof.

St George's. Sunlight falling red and blue on a stub hand.

The straycat cowfarm. White mucous hands. Blood-specked sows.

The frog-green pool at the Groot Drakenstein games club.

⌒

Peejay unzips his bag so that we can both lie on it in his canvas tent. The canvas smells faintly of straydog pee. An old tartan picnic rug covers us and it scratches with blackjacks and burs embedded in its fabric. But it is good to feel Peejay so close while the cold stars stud the black sky through the open flap.

Peejay is a man in my eyes. He lives life raw and rides fate like a wave. As for me, I duck out of the way and fear fins.

There were carefree times on the farm and at school, but fear always recurred. Fear of being dragged down by drowned hands, of a rat scraping up my shin, of being baited on the bus or being caned by mamba canes.

And now, there is the inescapable, gnawing dread of being caught by the sarmajoor. In my mind he has become the hairy, fiery-eyed tokoloshe, hellbent on finding me, on drawing my blood dry.

# Nahoon

We drive out of Jay Bay as a misty sun comes up over a moody sea.

We stop in Port Elizabeth for breakfast on a bleak, deserted beachfront. The wind rips off the sea and seagulls fly into the wind over the rocks without making headway.

In Port Elizabeth I draw my savings for a standby ticket overseas. I know it is like leaving a spoor in the sand for the police to find.

I offer Peejay money for the cords and sandals and to chip in for the ride.

– Forget it. Maybe one day I'll land on your doorstep, he says.

I wonder, as we drive along the winding coastal road, where my doorstep will be.

We go through the Ciskei: gothic aloes stabbing skyward through the stones.

Outside Port Alfred, a colony of white birds fills a dead black tree standing in a pool of saltwater by the roadside. The water level has dropped through the summer and the tree has surfaced like an unearthed skeleton. A heron weaves on spindly stilts through roots reaching up out of the mud like dead men's fingers.

Port Alfred: sulking fishing boats on the Kowie, under a half-moon bridge.

As we reach the outskirts of East London there is a black man in a black suit walking ahead of a woman who carries a suitcase on her head. On top of the suitcase is a wire cage with two white chickens inside and on top of the cage is a three-legged firepot. The sight reminds me of that German fable about the rooster that stands on the cat that stands on the dog that stands on the donkey.

We cross the Buffalo River and look down on the string of yachts moored in the harbour and, beyond them, the cargo ships and cobalt sea.

We park down by the paved seafront walk and get take-away pies and Freezeland milkshakes and watch disillusioned penguins wilt under the obscured sun. An old man in a frayed tweed jacket and bared skinny legs peers into rock pools, like some awkward, earthbound stork. A turbanned Xhosa woman with tobacco-stained teeth sells baskets and beads. I buy beads from her, thinking it will be good to have something tangibly African if I make it to the hazy world of overseas.

After slurping the milkshakes down, we head down to Nahoon Reef.

Nahoon: a rock shaped like a tortoise juts out into the Indian Ocean. High dunes spine along the beach to where the Nahoon River runs into the sea. There are a few surfers out by the tortoise head, and as we watch them skim the waves, the sun rips through the clouds and we see dolphins in the glare. On the radio Bob Marley sings *Three Little Birds* and, for the moment, the barbed wire and ostriches of Oudtshoorn are far, far away.

– A good omen, tunes Peejay.

Does he mean the dolphins, or the three little birds, or the sun?

While Peejay surfs I walk along the beach and climb the dunes where those stubby plants grow that you rub on a bluebottle sting. On the dunes I just catch the sound of Creedence Clearwater seeping through the radio static of the waves. I unbutton the lumberjack shirt and cords and lie there in army-issue underpants and Peejay's sandals and doze in the sun.

*Dolphins weave through the sky above the sighing stone pines. Then I see that the pines are full of Egyptian geese and the branches bend under the birds. The geese face north and then, as if a gun sounded, they begin to lift into the sky. The geese eclipse the sun and the unearthly whistle of their wings fills my head. They fly so low over me that sometimes the tips of their wings brush my face.*

I awake to find a silhouetted boy twiddling a feather in his fingers.

– I thought I should wake you before you burnt, he says.

He lies close by on a towel with a motif of oranges and lemons.

– I am Michelangelo.

– As you see, I am not David, I remark as I pull on my cords.

Michelangelo smiles at my shame over my bizarre tan.

– You travelling? He wonders.

– Yes.

– Lucky you. I'm still at school. When I get out I'm going to study drama at Rhodes. Then I'll go into film. This English teacher, Mister Ford, got me hooked on acting. He cast me as Nick in a play he wrote, based on *The Great Gatsby*. Do you act?

– No.

Michelangelo lip-ices his lips. Bubblegum flavour.

– Some afternoons I went over to Mister Ford's flat. He filmed me being Nick. Daisy was a mop and Jordan a golf bag. He made me act just in my Speedo. At first it felt weird in front of a teacher, but he sensed I had to kill my fear. That's how intuitive Mister Ford is. In the end it felt so *destined*.

He digs his toes down under the sand.

– *Destined*.

– I met a girl not so long ago and it felt like destiny. Now I'm not so sure.

– So what happened to her?

I waver, then gamble on telling him.

– I got my call-up.

– Oh, so that's why you have a panda tan.

– And that's why I'm wearing these army underpants.

– Oh. I just thought you had no taste.

– Thanks.

Michelangelo offers me a Camel and I cup it in my hands to light it in the breeze. I dangle it casually from my lips like my father does with his Texans but just get smoke in my eyes.

– Hey, says Michelangelo. If you could do anything, anything in the world, what would you do?

– I would live on the edge of the sea with Zelda, the café girl.

– You're a deserter. Aren't you? says Michelangelo, changing tack.

– I am.

– Was it so bad? says Michelangelo, pinching his toes.

– It was for me. Anyway, I jumped the wire and got a lift to East London. I hope to get a flight out of South Africa tomorrow.

– Shit, so this is like your last day on the beach?

– My last day under the sun.

I bury my feet in the sand.

# baleka baleka

Peejay drives me up Beach Road to the highway. There, amid the shreds and strips of bamboo of the roadside basket weavers, we say goodbye.

– Adios, says Peejay, with a hug and a rub of my head.

– So long, I say.

He waits in the Beetle in the shade, to make sure I get a lift. I hear snatches of Juluka from the motorcar radio. I have barely begun to hitch when a dented Dodge pulls up. The driver is a big black man in a Bogart hat and a Hawaiian shirt that pulls taut over his bongo drum of stomach.

– How far?

– Durban.

– I can get you through the Transkei.

– Thanks.

I turn to wave to Peejay.

In the Dodge: Elvis dangles from the rearview mirror. Fake cowskin hides the seats. Turns out the man is called Jomo.

Jomo loves my story of my fiddlefooting it out of Oudtshoorn. He bids me tell the part of the sarmajoor and the bulb over and over again. When we get near the Transkei border, he hides me in the boot under a doghair blanket.

The Dodge comes to a halt at the border post. In the boot I lie dead still. A scared foetus in a dry steel womb. The stink of dog in my nostrils and the bang of blood in my skull.

I make out Jomo's undulating voice, in Afrikaans. And another Afrikaans voice, blunt and laconic. I hear a tinny clang. Maybe a shoe against a hub. I wait for the boot to jaw apart and hard hands to jerk me out into torchlight. Instead, the motor coughs to life again.

On the other side of the Kei River, after a long curving climb away from the border post, Jomo frees me from the boot and laughs full and deep at having outwitted the South African Police.

As my fear subsides, I look out over the dashboard of the Dodge on the falling darkness and think of how fruitful the Groot Drakenstein valley is against this grazed-down land where the rains gouge dongas out of the earth.

– Like the scars of childbirth on a woman's hips, Jomo tunes, then laughs at my discomfort.

I know I am the reason for the pink wavy lines on my mother's hips. Lines with sheen to them, like mother-of-pearl.

– Have you never had a woman?

– Once. On the beach in Muizenberg.

– A lekker white girl on your white beach, hey?

His bongodrum stomach jellies with laughter. He is enjoying himself, old Jomo.

Just on the other side of Umtata, an oncoming motorcar flicks its headlamps at us. Damn, a roadblock. My heart beats wildly.

But again Jomo is in fits, for it turns out it is just another motorcar with a Kokstad numberplate. Just being friendly.

When Jomo drops me outside Kokstad, he tunes:

– Run boy run. Baleka baleka. But you will not escape Africa. It is in your bones and your blood.

A white couple from the town pick me up in an old avocado-green Benz. They are heading for Zinkwazi Beach along the south coast road and will drop me off in Durban. To avoid having to tell my story I feign sleep while a felt dog nods his head in the back window. Through squinted eyes I read the signs: Ifafa Beach. Umkomaas. Amanzimtoti. Durban.

# deck chair

Durban. Taxis, bicycles and rickshaws and the cries of papersellers. Neon lights in rain-shimmer streets. My last night in the land I was born in, perhaps forever. Two hours inland lies the farm. Is Beauty still living in the backyard hut? Is Jamani still at school with all the *unrest* and the burning of black schools? For a moment I wish I could be papoosed tutuzela tutuzela on Beauty's back again, or that I could be with Zane inside the woodstove kitchen while Lucky Strike weaves the magic strands of his stories. I wish I could smell my mother and hear my father say:

– Bona wena kosasa. See you tomorrow.

I wish I had Grandpa Barter's pocket knife in my pocket. All I have is the string of Xhosa beads I finger. The beads carry me into the past: I am again the barefoot, clay-smeared boy hunting lizards and catching fish in the likkewaan river with Zane and Jamani. I hear the nkankaan cry *ha ha haaa*. I hear Lucky Strike call: Fly fly fly, young baas.

The chug and rev of engines, the laughter of hatted figures dodging the falling rain, tugs me back to reality.

In the charged, humid nightfall, folk head for flickering bars and fizzing cafés, for theatre and romance.

My way winds down to Point Road and I walk along it until

hotels and flats give way to warehouses. Cranes and masts criss-cross in a blurred frieze in the rain. Grandpa Barter once said my mother went to the Cliff Richard dance looking like a Point Road whore, so I look for girls who match the image of a whore in my head: high heels, black fishnet stockings and painted lips, but I see none like that.

There is a pale girl, hair gone all stringy in the rain, eyeing me. I cannot tell how old she is. Maybe nineteen. I stand still in the humid rain, and she stares her haunting eyes at me.

– Hey sweetie. Want a fuck or a suck?

She says it so lazily that she might just as well have said: Want a Fanta or a Sprite?

I climb narrow stairs after her, up and up into an attic room with faded pink wallpaper and a red blanket on the bed that re-minds me of Grandmama Rudd's bloodred gown. The room feels bleak to me and the memory of Grandmama does not make me feel sexy. There is no music to create a mood, just the rain against the window.

– What's your name, sweetie?

I lie, as if she might be dragged into the dock by the sarmajoor to witness against me if she knew my name.

– Mine's Doris, she says as she deftly undoes my cords so that they flop down to my sandalled feet.

The name Doris reminds me again of my Grandmama and of times when women were called Doris or Marjorie or Ruby. Doris bids me lie on the red bed. My cords still folded around my feet, I hobble across the scabby carpet.

I look up into her eyes, feeling guilty that I feel so unsexy. Her unhooked breasts swing against my ribs, and I wish I had paid her to have a coffee with me instead.

Out of the blue, jazz floats up from a window below and mixes with rain-blurred voices and I close my eyes to float with the music. But I still see her stringy hair and haunting eyes. I want to cry over her old woman's name.

As it turns out, my last human encounter in South Africa is as impotent as my life in South Africa has been. I ran into a pole while running away from the police. I went to the army rather than face jail. And now I run from the army into the arms of a woman and my cock goes limp.

I do up my cords in shame.

– Never mind, says Doris. Another time.

⌒

Me in the taxi to the airport, running towards my bee-zithering dream of seeing the world at the end of the Atlantic, into the unknown.

crying for my mother and father, my brother

guilty for having sinned with a whore

guilty for leaving behind faceless and furtive encounters with black Africans. My white eyes averted. I never asked Mila how many children he had in the Transkei. I did not know his Xhosa name. Though Nana made my bed for all my Paarl years I never went inside her house. Once, from the door to her house, I glimpsed a museum of thrown-out things from ours:

a broken riempie stool, resting on bricks

earless china cups

a chipped coffee mug with the Paarl Boys' High emblem

a deck chair with a gaping hole in the canvas.

# yin yang

The tunnel is cold like death. The man at immigration curt. I tell him I am visiting family, for there are still relic strands of family in Gloucestershire and Edinburgh. He casts his eyes down me and I wriggle my bare toes inside Peejay's sandals. Flotsam washed up from the colonies.

The Underground. Rattling through nowhere. And then misted brick houses with small backyards and a horizon of chimneys. And then black again. I play with pound coins in my hand, feel their foreign heaviness. Gloucester Road. South Kensington. Knightsbridge. Green Park. Piccadilly Circus. I surface like a mole and the cold swoops down on me, a bird of prey beating its vast wings about my head.

As I child I believed there was a carnival circus at Piccadilly full of dancing bears and clowns and the works. Instead there is just a roundabout and a wall of neon flowers calmly unfurling tropical colours amid the jangle of London: Fosters blue and Coca-Cola red and Carlsberg green. The colours fill my eyes for a moment and then die, then fan out again. Through misted breath I watch the black cabs jam and jockey like gloss-scarabed dung-beetles.

Some guys in black leather with lime green and pink hair

shake up beer cans and spray beer foam at Eros. One guy, with a nose ring like the bull that trod me into the dung, snarls at me when he catches me watching. This is another England from the country Grandpa Barter told me of.

It begins to rain on a pavement painting of Bob Marley. The colours run and the dreadlock artist gives up, tips a tin of coins onto the pavement and fingers through them. Just as a Zulu sangoma tells the future, by the fall of bones and stones. The artist flips one coin aside, and when he is gone I pick it up. It is Spanish, with a hole in it. I pocket it.

The chill seeps into my bones. My bare toes ache as if the ice-cold Clifton sea is washing over my feet. My ears burn with cold. I am afraid of the hovering, cruel-beaked cold.

I escape into a sport and outdoor shop on the Circus and buy wool hiking socks. I hate the scratch of the wool on my skin but the man says wool is just the thing for the cold. He says I will want a fleece. I imagine he means a sheep skin but he gives me a kind of tracksuit top to zip up to my chin. He tells me it has been tried out on Himalayan climbing expeditions.

The man reckons I will surely need hiking boots to combat the cold, and though I want them I am scared of running out of money, so I say I am fine with my sandals. He wants to know where I am from, and when I say South Africa he nods as if I had said Timbuktu and it explains the sandals and all. Still, he calls me sir when I hand the heavy pound coins to him.

When I come out of the shop the rain has dried up. I walk down to Leicester Square, dodging puddles so as not to drench my hiking socks. Where I had imagined Leicester Square fringed by arty cafés and bars, there is McDonald's and Burger King and Häagendazs. A busker mimics the clockwork doll walk of Charlie Chaplin. It makes me smile and then it begins to rain again.

A flock of chittering Spanish chicas run for the shelter of a
film theatre to lick Häagendazs. Outside the theatre a sad, sallow
beggar huddles in the rain, rocking on his heels like Birdy gone
Vietnam-crazy. One of the girls drops her tub of Häagendazs into
his begging hands and the others giggle.

I take shelter in a callbox and read the advertisements for exotic Thai and blonde Swedish girls before picking up the mouth-
piece. At the foot of Africa, at the foot of the Simonsberg, the
albinofrog telephone calls its shrill croak through the house. Nana
picks up the phone and wails when she hears it is me, as if my
voice comes from the grave. Her wails set the dogs howling. I drop
another fruitless coin into the slot before my mother comes to the
phone. I tell her I am fine and am calling from Leicester Square.
My mother's crying mixes with the background howling and the
*clank clank* of the telephone devouring coins.

– Don't cry, Mom. I'm okay. You know I always dreamed of
London.

I look through the rain-beaded glass at huddled shapes rush-
ing by under hoods and black umbrellas. I run out of coins and
my mother is cut short as she begins to tell me about the police
having been there.

Afterwards, I walk down to Trafalgar Square in the rain and
mope around in the lee of a stone lion. High above my head
Nelson surveys the pigeon-riddled square while red buses skid
around the rim. Outside South Africa House, rain-drenched pro-
testers stand on the pavement like a straggling, forlorn flock of
crows. The ink on some hand-painted banners bleeds, so that you
can only just make out: *Free Mandela*.

From Trafalgar I wander down to Big Ben and stand on the
bridge and look up and down the river as wide as the Orange,
but tinted green instead of saffron. On the square in front of Big

Ben I see Jan Smuts cast in bronze. In history at Paarl Boys' High I was taught that he was a traitor to the Afrikaners for taking South Africa into the war against Hitler, on the side of the English who had burnt their farms and taken their women and children to the concentration camps.

As I walk along the Thames, I begin to feel the adventure of being alone in London. I have no past here. No one knows that I kissed Bulldog on the bus, or that I was a moffie deserter. One thing is for sure, I will never be called a rooinek in London.

To escape the biting cold I go into a building called The Tate where they advertise a free art film. The film has already run for a while and I do not understand it, but I gradually recover feeling in my fingers. For about a quarter of an hour the camera focuses on a round form. At first I think it is a sand dune, but then I see the bellybutton. It is a stomach full of unborn baby, a stomach as big as Jomo's bongo drum. Now and then a mothwing shadow drifts over the stomach, but otherwise nothing happens that I am aware of.

A man in a uniform shakes me awake and says they are closing. I think it is the army and that the sarmajoor has tracked me down and I run a few steps, before it sinks in that I am in London.

I walk back down to the Chelsea bank, and along the cold, misty river to Charing Cross, where folk cab cosily to theatres.

I walk through the crushed fruit fallen from the daytime barrows of Berwick Street and go into a Soho pub. I order some beer and it is tapped into a deep glass by the young barman. *Wild Thing* thumps though the boxes.

I stand by the fire. Mist smokes off Peejay's cords. *Wild Thing* is chased by a deep voice rapping *pasties and a G-string, beer and a shot.*

I sip the night away on the same flat pint of Carlsberg by the fire. Above the fireplace hang old sepia photographs of cricket teams.

One afternoon at the Groot Drakenstein Games Club, 6 000 miles south of Soho, my father said to me: Life is like a cricket ball. One side scuffed and grazed. One side rubbed smooth. When life is hard, remember that the ball swings around again.

The faces in the bar remain distant, as if I am watching another art film without any meaning I can discern.

I keep drifting back to the afternoon I rode the bus along the edge of the sea with Zelda: the tints of sunlight in her hair and the merry clink of the wine bottles.

On the beach Zelda's stomach bowstrings taut under my fingers. As longing ripples through me, doves, not Cape turtledoves but white Picasso doves, flutter out of her sex into a blood-orange sky.

The bar empties after eleven. As I turn to go, the barman says:

– You South African?

– Yes. How'd you know?

– I picked up the accent when you ordered beer. Besides, I knew you weren't English the moment you asked for a glass of beer instead of a pint of lager. I'm Delarey, he says as he shakes my hand over the bar.

– Incredible I should meet a South African on my first day in England.

Maybe I had not drifted all the way into the realm of random things after all.

– Hell, Delarey laughs, half the bloody barmen in London are

South Africans or Ozzies. Listen, I have a room upstairs. It's spartan but you can kip on the floor if you like.

I clearly give out the impression I have nowhere to go. I had thought of asking a taxidriver if he knew of a cheap hotel.

– Give me a hand with the glasses and we'll go for a coffee, unless you're too buggered after the flight and all.

– I'd love to go for a coffee.

– Good. Maybe I can lend you a pair of shoes? What size are you?

So we end up in a coffee shop in Soho where they brew Italian espresso and you can look through the breath-misted windows at a pink neon sign on the other side of Dean Street that flashes: GIRLS GIRLS GIRLS. Under the neon sign a woman perches on a barstool in a doorway and gestures to the men who walk by. Men with wives or girlfriends steal glances at her zipped miniskirt, others let their eyes drink in her stockinged legs.

After the coffee, Delarey and I queue outside a café called Freestyle until some whim tickles the bouncer to let us past his bulk. Inside we get bottled Budweiser at the bar. It costs five pounds. You can get a whole crate of beer for five pounds in South Africa. Not Budweiser or Carlsberg, because of the boycotts, but good beer.

– Hard to find a beer after the pubs shut, so you fork out the pounds, Delarey says.

The lights flicker colours across faces and I see two boys kissing deeply. When the music dims between songs I can hear the sucking. One of the boys playfully blows a kiss at me when he catches me gawking. Delarey laughs when my cheeks go red.

I hold the cold beer to cool my face as Delarey tells me of his plans to save pounds in London then head for Paris and Rome and Paros.

I stay with Delarey above the Soho pub. In the evenings I sit on a barstool and read Kerouac's surreal travels across America. When I surface from my book I find Delarey has tapped another free pint of beer for me. During the day I look for jobs in cafés and bars and bookshops in Camden and Notting Hill Gate and South Kensington, but I am turned away time and time again because I have no work visa. I begin to feel worthless and that I will end up begging in Leicester Square like the Birdy man.

I sip slow coffees at Café LaVille, on a bridge over a canal, looking down on the vividly painted boats that float out from under me, reminding me of fishing boats in Kalk Bay. But in London there are no barefoot coloured boys dangling handlines into the water. I see lone fishermen fish from the bank of the barge-path to Camden, but I never see anyone catch a fish. I peer into a bucket, hoping to see a fish or two. Instead the bucket is full of maggots. The fisherman dips his hands into the maggots and scatters them over the water for the fish, just like a farmer flinging seeds over the earth.

Afternoons: I explore the kaleidoscope of Camden Lock with all its ceramics and sarongs and exotic carpets and bolts of Indian cloth. I stand dazed on street corners before choosing a road for no other reason than I have never walked it before. Making a pound last the whole afternoon by wandering aimlessly for hours before going into Freud's for another bitter black coffee. I watch films for one pound twenty at a cinema behind Leicester Square, where it merges into China Town. Sometimes I hide in the toilets and come out when the next film begins.

In spite of free beer and cheap films I am skint after a fortnight. Delarey, sounding just like Peejay, tunes:

– Just be cool, something will pitch.

But I am not so sure. The cricket ball is swinging slowly. I am down to my last twenty pounds and sick of the cheddar and pickle sandwiches Delarey smuggles upstairs for me, when I pick up one of the free magazines you find on street corners in London. Listlessly flipping through it, an advert catches my eye:

Chambermaid wanted in quaint harbourside country hotel, Lynmouth, North Devon. Room provided.

I call up the hotel from a callbox in Gloucester Road.

– Hello, I'm calling from London about the chambermaid job. I was wondering if it was still free.

– Actually, says a voice sounding all Olivier, we had a girl in mind.

– I understand, I say, my heart plunging. It's just that I thought you might give me a chance. I was in the army so I can make a bed and scrub toilets and iron and that kind of thing. You see, I need the job.

– Are you Australian? the hotelkeeper wonders.

– South African. My folks live on a wine farm near Cape Town.

– Which farm? I may know it as I've visited South Africa a few times. Good trout fishing you know.

– Boschendal, I tell him.

– Boschendal? I lunched there under the pines. Say, do you play tennis?

– I do.

– Do you have a racquet with you?

– I never go anywhere without my tennis racquet.

– Well then, you hop on the evening train to Exeter and I'll have our chef, Jimi, come down to fetch you. We'll play tennis and I daresay we'll think of something for you to do.

☞

My mother's brother once took me fly fishing as a small boy. I tangled the line again and again and almost hooked a cow before I felt a fish tug. I reeled it in and saw a black-spotted shimmer of fish for a fraction of time, before it broke the line. It haunts me to think of a fish somewhere under the black waters with my steel hook in its gills. Like a shameful memory deep down among the mudooze reeds. Like a dog down a well shaft.

☞

I catch the Exeter train from Waterloo with a Camden rucksack woven in Kathmandu, and a wooden racquet from Oxfam so old Fred Perry might have played with it. Delarey is there at Waterloo to lend me the money I am short of for the ticket and to wave goodbye.

On the way to Exeter I see the England I had imagined before arriving in London. Black-and-white cows like graphic art against a green so green it is hard for the eye to absorb. I see Salisbury cathedral lance into a sky as milky as a blind eye.

At the Dorset station of Templecombe the train halts for a long time. Word from the front is that we have killed a cow and they are dragging it off the tracks. I wonder what drove a cow surrounded by vast green fields to graze on the railway line. The dead cow on the tracks reminds me of when the school bus was on a roundabout in Paarl and a policeman on a bike came by on the inside. The tyres skidded and the policeman's head went under the bus. The bus jammed to a halt and the kids who had seen the slide yelled. The coloured bus driver climbed out and walked down the side of the bus, then fell down flat in the road. The policeman lay under the bus but you could see the blood flow slow as candlewax towards the gutter. We sat in the canned heat until they covered the blood with sand and a policeman drove the bus on through Paarl to drop us off on the farms.

We reach Exeter as black ink seeps into the sky.

Jimi is there, smoking a cigarette against an MG convertible. You can tell he wants me to think he is cool with his fag and wheels. On the winding road up to Lynmouth, through Barnstaple, Jimi tunes:

– You into pool at all?

– No.

I have only played carom, Indian finger pool, on the veranda with Zane.

– I'll teach you to shoot some pool. At night, after the chaos of the kitchen, we head up to a pub where there's pool and good bitter. Though you South Africans drink cold lager like the Ozzies, yeah?

I confess to loving beer ice-cold.

– There's a barman there who fancies himself as a philosopher. Don't be fazed if he corners you. He comes on to all the new boys in town.

I play tennis with the hotelkeeper on the edge of the sea. A gust blows across the channel and you can just make out Wales with its factory chimneys on the far side. My Oxfam racquet twangs like an untuned guitar. The wind and my instinct to cut the ball send it drifting out of his reach all the time. He is as flummoxed by my unorthodox curving of the ball as the English soldiers in the Boer War were by the Boer tactics of hiding and shooting from undercover.

– I am used to a tradition of tennis, he says after the game, where the ball has good length and one has a fair chance of returning it.

I think I have dashed my chances of a job and will be hitching back to Delarey for cheese and pickle sandwiches like a begging dog.

But he's forgiving.

– If you can scour pots like you can spin a ball, there's a job as kitchen porter for you.

So I become a kitchen boy in Devon in a thatch timber-framed hotel that existed as a hotel long before Jan van Riebeeck sailed from Holland to the Cape. I scour pots and pans in a cramped room under a fly-specked bulb, a dim reminder of the sun. I swab the floor. I steelwool the stove. I endlessly peel potatoes, for the English love their chips. I hose down the hotelkeeper's Labrador after it has rolled in cow dung. I behead and gut trout that slither out of my hands so that I cut my fingers instead. I barter crayfish from the fishing boats and haul them to the hotel in a basket, like the wicker baskets the coloureds in the Cape fill with picked fruit.

The crayfish (which the English call lobsters) always try to climb out of the basket, as if they sense their macabre fate. One crayfish pincers my finger to the bone before I can fling it against the harbour wall. The shell cracks open like the crab the coloured boy stoned against the tar.

I have to tip the basket of crayfish into a pot of scalding water. My blood shivers with the guilt as their shells change colour from black to red. Not postbox red. Not cockscomb red. But pink red like eggs stained at Easter with a drop of the blood of Jesus.

With a butcher knife I cleave the crayfish down the middle and prize out their white flesh. Sometimes the shells explode as I knife down and I end up with bits of crayfish in my hair and everywhere. And if the bell rings I drop the crayfish and run to the front desk, my hair specked with crayfish and my apron flecked with trout blood.

Old ladies pay me 50 pence to cart their suitcases up the rickety, winding stairs to some far corner of the hotel. Had they glimpsed the blood and carnage in my viewless room behind the kitchen, where trout and crayfish heads eye me from a barrel, they might not find Devon so quaint.

Still, I escape the crayfish and the old ladies on my long afternoon runs along the coastal path that winds past an abbey and down to the cove of Woody Bay. During the war a German plane came down on a hill above Woody Bay. Farmers armed with pitchforks captured the pilot. Like him, I have landed in a land of foreigners who spend long hours staring soulfully into their bitter and who play pool and darts and say cryptic things, like *tor* for hill and *combe* for valley.

At night Jimi helps me swab the floors so we can leave the hotel together and race uphill in his MG to the pub that spans the river. The gay barman there pours a cold Stella for me as soon as I come in, and I sit at the bar and shoot the breeze. I call him Camus. My Stella never runs dry as long as I have an ear for his philosophy.

Some afternoons I run along the high road across the moor to Porlock. It was on this road that Coleridge found Xanadu, *where Alph, the sacred river, ran down to a sunless sea. A savage place under a waning moon, haunted by a woman wailing for her demon-lover.* But that stranger tapping at the door popped the dream and Coleridge never could find the way back.

Whenever I run along the Porlock Road I recall my Xanadu at the foot of Africa: Groot Drakenstein, dragon mountain, and the Berg River flowing through the vineyard valley down to the cold Atlantic. And I wonder if I will ever see the savage and enchanted valley bathed in blood orange again, or if I will live forever in exile beyond Xanadu.

And at night Dylan and Neil Young unreel time and again in the pub over the river.

And at night *Tangled Up in Blue* unreels time and time again in the pub over the river. Bougainvillaea tangled up in morning glory. A mind entangled in the past.

Camus believes the present contains the past.

– You will find all the conflicts and passions of history in this town at this time, on a reduced scale and in a diluted form, he murmurs, burrowing his fingers into his beard.

It is absurd to me that all of history should be reduced to the small town of Lynton, North Devon, but it is original as a philosophy. My only philosophy is my father's homespun wisdom that life is like a cricket ball. Two hemispheres. Smooth female yin and grazed male yang.

Pool: Jimi tells me to relax my fingers and glide the cue, not jab at the white ball. But still the balls ricochet in random directions.

There is a girl Jimi fancies, Marina, half-Venezuelan, half-French. She works in the rival hotel on the rocks across the harbour. Jimi bends over her to ensure she has a good stance for pool, while the old men at the bar wink knowingly at each other.

One of the old men is a sheep farmer with leathery skin and beer foam lingering on his moustache and his sheepdog at his feet.

As if a lost Zulu sangoma roving the black moors of Devon has cast a spell on him, he turns into a poet in the pub and lovingly describes those balls of bone and skin that owls gob up.

– You rub the ball between your fingers until it crumbs in your hands and there you have a life story in your palm.

After the pub shuts, I lie in my bed over the harbour and listen to the tide roll the stones on the shore and to the clink of rigging against masts. I think of the valley and of Zelda and sometimes the two mingle like bloodbrother blood.

Dam water beading on her skin, she holds me after Maljan shamed me in the PT changing rooms.

On the garage roof, among the pumpkins, her salt tears sting my broken skin after Visoog Vorster caned me.

On this shore, in the old days, land pirates used to lure storm-tossed ships onto the rocks with lamps and illusions of rescue and then ransack the splintered boats before they sank.

Here, at the foot of England, I lose myself in the ritual of bartering for crayfish, the long runs along the sea or across the moor, Camus' cold Stella and philosophic meanderings. But when, out of the blue, I hear Eddie Grant sing *Give me Hope, Joanna* on the radio, Africa shivers through my blood like a reflex shrinking of the balls.

I hear a boy and girl flirt in Afrikaans on the harbour wall at sunset. An English sunset: tepid orange, like white wine from black grapes. Wine denied time to draw the red from the skins. The boy and girl seem so carefree and uncluttered by the past that I let them be. I go back into the windowless room with my bruised-fruit bitterness, wishing for a blood-orange sunset. Undiluted, flaming blood orange. The sunset that ends another day of a man footing after a Firestone tyre from Paarl to Groot Drakenstein to Franschhoek.

When Africa ripples through me I see the tusk-white house under the Simonsberg, and the Berg River wind through the valley. I recall the taste of udderhot milk, the sweet juice of hand-plucked peaches, and the orange teardrops you find when you peel the skin off a wedge of orange. I even see the outline of Africa in rain puddles and in the foam of my pee in the toilet bowl. For me Africa does not end in Morocco. I hear and see its echoes everywhere.

Mister Slater taught me that Jung travelled away from the time-bound mindworld of Switzerland to find the buried self of timeless raw instinct in Africa: so raw he could smell the blood that had seeped into the land. In England all the land is tamed and I yearn for the wild veld.

I have roots in England. My forefathers traded in fish fished out of this same Bristol Channel. And have I not been teased all my Paarl Boys' days for being a rooinek Englishman? Yet I do not feel at all English. I am a homesick kaffirboetie who misses the sound of Xhosa, that unending river of clicks, and the smell of the dust that creeps into sandals and hides between toes.

And I miss black faces. Mila. Nana. The hobbling man at the BP garage at Simondium, who always wipes the windows and checks the tyres and water, knowing my mother will give him a Christmas box. The women who pack purchases into bags at the Spar. The men who wash your motorcar while it is parked in the sun, for two rand. The barefoot schoolboys who trade handmade wire bicycles and windmills at the crossroads in Klapmuts.

Strange that I should feel so English in Africa and dream of Europe, and so foreign in England and long for Africa again.

*Soutpiel*, Maljan would call me. My salty cock dangling in the Atlantic.

Still, it is good to be free from the yoke of unbending rules I have lived under in South Africa.

Don't keep snakes under your desk. Don't chatter like bloody mousebirds in class or you will get the ruler. Don't bleed ink on your textbooks or you will get the cane. Don't walk around with your blazer unbuttoned, even if the sun blazes down, or you will be for the high jump. Shave your hair. Shine your shoes. Stand in rows when the bell goes for school.

Don't pee in a non-white toilet, even if you have to pinch. Don't go into the post office through the non-white door, or the lady with the bun on her head will snap at you. Don't sit on a non-white bench, even if it is free or if it happens to be the only shady bench, for the police are on the lookout for such blackbench boys. Don't go into the third-class compartment of a train, for only non-whites have the right to travel third class.

I break. The balls scatter, ricochet, but not one heads for a hole. I hand Jimi the cue. He chalks it with blue chalk while his eyes dart around the green felt. There is a smirk on his lips. I can tell he is going for the kill.

His first shot sends a ball flying down a far pocket. I can't bear to watch him clean up, so I turn to Marina, Jimi's girl, and tell her of all the things forbidden in South Africa.

– Oh you poor thing, just imagine not even having the freedom to sit on any bench that is free, goes Marina.

Put that way, and after a few beers, it does seem that I suffered unduly.

In Devon the hedges are so high they obscure the view, but as I run I have sudden glimpses of Van Gogh grass through gaps. Then blurred hedge again. It is like looking through a viewfinder that goes blank between frames, then drops into focus.

I see a flat hedgehog on the road and it reminds me of a story Granny Barter told of how, when she was a little girl in Gloucestershire, she found a hedgehog in the snow and thought it was dead. Her mother put it in the oven until it uncurled from its deep sleep.

I glance over my shoulder as I run through Lynton, up on the hill above Lynmouth, half expecting to see the spluttering, raving sarmajoor with Boyd in tow. The sarmajoor blundering through Dorset, a baboon in a tea-room.

Camus asks me why I ran from the army:

– For political reasons?

– Yes.

I lie. I ran because I was scared the sarmajoor would drill me dead into the dust.

– Hmmm. Will you stay on at the hotel as a kitchen porter or do you have other plans?

– I dream of seeing the world.

It sounds cheeky coming from the no-visa guy who beheads trout and murders crayfish in-between bellhopping for old ladies.

– Then what the fuck are you doing in Devon? laughs Camus.

– I think your dream's cool, says Marina.

– Your dream would have to be devoid of a plan to be truly existentialist, Camus adds.

Jimi just says:

– Set 'em up. I'll break.

So I set up the balls, knowing full well he will beat me hollow again. Jimi breaks the balls so wildly that the white flies off the green felt and cracks a pint glass that bleeds black Guinness across the bar. Camus hardly glances up, so absorbed is he in enlighten- ing us on existentialism:

– It is when the same day spins out forever.

No doubt in the same town, I think to myself.

– And all experience is equal. Peeing beer into the urinal is just as significant as painting a canvas, or making love.

There's an old fisherman in Lynmouth, known to all as Jo-the- Fish. There's Jo-the-Fish and Jim-the-Spade, who tends the flowers (and who once dug up the corpse of a young girl who was buried behind the inn without her head).

His sheepdog is always on his heels, a dogged shadow. Jo-the- Fish trades fish for a beer at the hotel and his dog curls up under his barstool during the long hours of gazing into the amber. He trades fish for ganja from a boat anchored in the fog of the Bristol Channel.

Down on the pebbled beach one night, Jo-the-Fish parcels out his magic by a driftwood fire. Flames dance in the eyes of the sheepdog as he gazes at his master. Marina holds her lighter to the resin in her fingers, then scratches it into a paper furrow, mixing it in with Javaanse Jongens tobacco.

# beach boy

A postcard of Nyhavn in Copenhagen comes with the hotel post. Jimi teases me because red lips kissed it over the handwriting. The letters slant like blades of grass in the wind. It is a reply to my postcard of Lynmouth harbour with the boats keeling on the mud at low tide, sent from Devon to Cape Town and forwarded from Cape Town to Denmark.

*My dear beach boy*

*I am back in Copenhagen. You remember when we met in the Blue Note Café and I was reading* Out of Africa *and you told me of your friend in Copenhagen? Well, here I sit in a café in Nyhavn and think of my South African and how hard it must have been in the army for you to run away. I wish you had run to Denmark. At night I work in a bar, called the Yellow Submarine. Mostly students come. I will always remember the beach in Hout Bay and the red wine on the sea.*

*Love*

*Zelda*

*PS. Maybe you will still come to Copenhagen. I hope so.*

– Sweet red lips for the beach boy. Howcome we never see you surf the Devon waves? Jimi taunts.

This plucks a raw chord, for I felt so uncool among the Jay Bay surfers with their bronzed bodies and tangled hair, gliding the long slow break while I peered into the shadows for sharks.

I keep the postcard folded in my pocket for days and days. I fish it out during the lulls in the kitchen. I know it like a liturgy. While the steam mists on the tiles above the sink and the steel-wool skins my fingers raw, I chant her name under my breath:

Zelda Zelda Zelda

vowels like dry mouths longing for rain.

Jo-the-Fish's sheepdog comes to the bar alone one night. He curls up under the barstool. He whines as dreaming dogs do.

In my dazed yearning I drop a scrapbook of my photographs and jotted-down images of Africa and love poems for Zelda into a rock pool. It dries on my windowsill but the pages warp wavily and it reminds me of the way stranded earthworms curl when they dry out in the African dust. I post the book to Zelda, because it smells of the sea and reveals my blurred-ink love, and pen a letter for her.

*Dear Zelda*

*I am still at my kitchen sink. The hotel is a tortoise-shell world that I could lose myself in but for my longing for you and the Groot Drakenstein valley. There are no mermaids here and there is no beach sand, but this is the same Atlantic*

*that flows into Hout Bay. I would love to see you in the*
*summer in Denmark once I have saved pounds. I may stay*
*in Copenhagen forever if the barmaids are good.*

*Love*
*Gecko, your beach boy*

Again Jo-the-Fish's sheepdog comes in alone and dozes under his ritual barstool. After I've mopped the kitchen, I skip the ride up to the pub on the hill. I walk along the beach to Jo-the-Fish's shack under a full moon. His dog follows me. The door is shut. Nailed to the door is the jaw of a fish. A window is ajar. The dog jumps onto a tipped-over wheelbarrow, then onto the sill and inside. I peer into the gloom. I make out a shadowy, headless form. As my eyes adjust I see Jo-the-Fish in a chair, his head slumped forward. A hand dangles to be licked by his dog. You'd think he was asleep, if not for the reek.

# old dog

Grandpa Barter, the man who played hockey for England and taught the prince of Siam, ended up in a madhouse on the flat plains south of Cape Town.

I went to visit him with my mother and Granny Barter in our old Peugeot 404. We stopped at a roadside stall under a torn Cinzano umbrella to buy some bananas. The coloured man wrapped the bananas in brown paper. I wished we had taken colourful flower-patterned paper along for Grandpa.

He was drugged and confused. My mother told me they ran charges through him to cure the longing for rum. The frame of his glasses had cracked and was fixed with a plaster that sponged up the oil from his nose. They took his teeth away in case he choked on them. His jowls hung slack and he drooled into the shirt pocket that used to be a quiver full of pencils for *The Cape Times* crossword. They took his pencils too, in case he stabbed himself or one of the mad ones, or the nurses.

Grandpa Barter, the word artist, slurred out words. Only Granny could decipher the sounds, from having followed him from Gloucestershire to Siam to Egypt to South Africa.

The mad ones sat with their heads cocked at a blaring TV, screwed up high on the wall, out of their reach. A bell rang and they all stood to walk haphazardly away, with the jilted TV yelling after them. Grandpa began to fidget restlessly as if he dared not defy the bell.

I helped my mother rock him to his feet and watched him shuffle down the long empty corridor. His head was bent and his trousers sagged. He reached behind to pull the fabric free of the cleft of his ass, where it had pinched from sitting.

– Grandpa, I called.

And he turned to look into my eyes, but no words came to me. Then he winked at me over the plaster rim of his glasses, as if to say: this old dog still has a trick or two up his sleeve. And for a fleeting moment he was the old Grandpa Barter who had made up the story of rescuing the Siamese princess and taught me to Indian dribble a hockey ball.

A few days later he fell hard and they sent him to Simondium to die under the Simonsberg in a teak deck chair he had made with his own hands. Perhaps, as he looked out over the vineyards towards Paarl Rock, he saw in his mind's eye, in the winking-eye of his young soul, the green Wye valley on the other side of the world.

Not long after he died, Granny Barter pined to death. Perhaps that was Grandpa's last trick, reeling her after him.

⌒

From my sink I hear a caterwauling from in front of the hotel. I run out with rolling pin in hand. On the harbourside a man is writhing on the stones, and two guys in Umbro football shirts are booting him in the ribs. Onlookers yell, beg, taunt. I hear the crack of a rib caving in. I bludgeon one of the boys over the head with the rolling pin. He sags to his knees. I drop the rolling pin and spin on my heels. I race along to the far end of the harbour wall, to the sea. The tide is out and the harbour too shallow. I race to the end of the harbour wall, to the open sea. I hear footfalls on my heels. As I reach the end, I dive.

I skin my chin on the pebbles before surfacing and clawing my way through the waves. In the corner of my eye stones arrow into the water. A stone stings my head. I dive under and blood smokes past my eye. I feel behind my ear and a flap of skin peels away from my skull. My jaw gapes to yell my fear and I gag on salt water. I come up spewing and spluttering. I tread water, flinching for fear of stones.

No stone falls. I blink blood out of my eyes. A policeman is chasing the stonethrower along the beach. Just as they reach Jo-the-Fish's shack, the sheepdog leaps up at the guy. He stumbles and the policeman rugby-tackles him. Outside the hotel the other guy, rubbing his rollingpinned head, is shoved into the back of a policevan. On the harbour wall folk stand, pointing out at me.

# Tianti

Jimi tells me the guys are out of jail, that they got off lightly as the one being booted had it coming to him. So I know they're out there, and that they've got it in for me. I run my fingers along the stitched centipede on my shaven head.

I sense it's time to run again.

In Covent Garden, the café umbrellas flower like hibiscus against the stone. A rastaman comes up the steps from the Underground toilets.

– Want some acid, brother? Get high for the cost of a pint.

– I'm not sure.

– Hey brother, you live until you die.

– Where you from?

– T an' T man.

– Tianti?

– Trinidad an' Tobago.

I give him two pounds and he gives me a corner of blotting paper, which he calls California Sunshine.

– Do I swallow it, the sunshine?

– Jesus. You melt it under your tongue.

He looks at me with pity in his eyes.

– Thanks. Goodbye.

– When I don't see you, I dream of you, he tunes.

I glance down at the bit of paper in my hand. When I look up again the rastaman is gone. I stand with it in my hand for a long time, feeling self-conscious and imagining that all the bobbies within a mile must smell it, like a shark smells blood, and be homing in on me. In the end, when no bobby comes, I put it under my tongue as the man said, and it feels dry and scratchy for a moment. I wade through the milling faces and colours of James Street and Neal Street, waiting for something to happen.

Down a narrow alley I find a hidden wedge of courtyard called Neal's Yard, and as I sip mango juice and pigeons flutter up into a yellow sky, the acid blooms in my head.

I stay a long time, holding the rim of the bobbing table, a buoy on a placid sea.

I tread the transparent water at Boulders while jackass penguins glide under me.

⌒

Revisiting Delarey's old bar in Soho, I see soundless footage of Soweto on a teevee screwed to the wall like the TV in the madhouse. David Bowie sings *China Girl* and I drink a pint. The tuneful song is out of synch with the images: *toyi-toyi dustfeet fists guns dogs blood sjamboks barricades and a burning bus with tyres in the sky*

Outside in Berwick Street I suck in the colour: yellow honeydew melons from Brazil, orange melons from Senegal.

– Beautiful ripe mangoes from Ireland, a fruitseller calls.

On the Underground from Leicester Square out to Heathrow I feel so bowed down by the blood and shit in South Africa. But as the train surfaces into the sunlight my mood picks up, for I am soon to see Lars, my pigeon-killing, gate-swinging idol, and Zelda of the sunflared hair and redwine breasts. A tube cowboy in snake-skin boots jumps on and strums Roger Miller's *King of the Road* on the guitar. Londoners dip deeper into their newspapers and books, but an old black man across from me instinctively taps his foot.

– Hi folks. Thanks for coming to my show. It's good of you to come. This next song is a song of hope. *I can see clearly now the rain is gone …*

The black man jumps to his feet and jousts his ivory-headed cane in the air as if it is a Zulu assegai.

The lady next to me pulls her skirt down further over her pink knees. Across from me a bank of newspapers hide the heads.

The tube-cowboy comes around with a sack, like a deacon gathering the collection in church. I drop in a coin and the black man empties his pockets.

– Running late folks. Got to do another show. You can come through if you want to.

He jumps out onto a deserted platform and, as the doors slice closed, his head pops up in the next car. You can just make out the tune of *King of the Road* seeping through.

⌒

There is a bus from the airport to the Copenhagen central station where Lars is waiting for me. He's not the type to reveal his feelings but I skip along at his heels as we walk past the gates of Tivoli through the crowded walkway to Nyhavn harbour. Tall men and women glide by like giraffes. Nyhavn is as pretty as the postcard image in my head: canvas umbrellas like wind-filled sails, dazzling white against the pastel houses and wooden ships and blue sky.

We get hotdogs from a windowed van and Carlsberg beer and feed bits of bread to black-headed seagulls.

We walk along the cobbled harbourside to see the mermaid, past ships moored to rusty rings. She too is as beautiful as in the postcards, but small and close to shore. I had imagined her being on a solitary island you could only reach by boat. As we arrive, tourists tumble out of a bus on to the harbourside and jump across to the rock to touch her and be photographed with her.

So many hands have rubbed her breasts that the bronze gleams like a piano pedal treaded over a lifetime.

– Her original head was sawn off by vandals, Lars tells me. It may be somewhere in the harbour.

Back in Nyhavn, Lars and I sit with our feet dangling over the wall like the Kalk Bay handline boys, drinking Carlsberg. I am excited to be in a place I dreamed of, but wish I hadn't seen the mermaid surrounded by tourists and that she still existed untouched in my imagination.

We dredge up stories of the farm and the dam and kebabed pigeons and Steely Dan. I tell him about how I found Zelda reading *Out of Africa* in the Blue Note Café, and how I fell head over heels for her. I tell him about the sarmajoor and the light bulb, about Peejay and the Jay Bay surfers. Lars smiles when I tell him about my kitchenboy flirts with crayfish and old ladies in Devon. It feels good to make him laugh and I want to hold his hand or something because he is so physical a reminder of the valley I pine for.

– You should become a storyteller, he laughs.

Lars knows I am dying to see Zelda and he shows me the way to the Yellow Submarine, past the round tower and up near the north station. Outside the bar, he tunes:

— Leave some of the Danish girls for me. I'll see you when I see you.

He takes my rucksack for me and gives me a key to his flat. Then he winks at me and walks away as coolly as if we still see each other most days just by crossing the road. Swinging on the gate under a blood-orange sunset. Nero and Fango barking at the squirrels in the stone pines. Tractors rattling by, the trailer bins filled with fruitpickers catching a lift home after a long day in the sun.

I go into the bar full of young folk drinking and chatting and peering through the smoke at backgammon boards and newspapers. *Hey Jude* on the jukebox.

I sit on a free barstool at the bar and look for Zelda as *Hey Jude* fades into *Strawberry Fields*.

Zelda is not there. Instead there is a waitress with black hair and black fingernails and skin so white her fingers look like piano keys, and a predatory panther look. She homes in on me to ask what I want. I want Zelda but I just order a beer.

*Big Yellow Taxi* comes over the jukebox. Not just the Beatles then. I fleetingly recall Che and Matanga and the Jamaica girls but my heart beats too fast for reverie. Zelda might happen at any time.

The panther comes back with my Carlsberg.

An Indian flowerseller with a white beard goes from table to table, but is ignored. Then he stands in front of me with his forlorn eyes staring into me as if he can see my naked feelings for Zelda, and pities me.

I feel as if all eyes are focused on me, like the old days on the school bus, and I buy one of his roses. He wants 20 kroner, the price of a beer, for just one rose. I dare not quibble, for how am I to know what a rose costs in Copenhagen?

Just then I see another waitress with a tray of beers balanced on one hand. She swings her hips as she weaves through the tables towards the rowdy far corner. They are strong blokes, like the boys in the back seat of the school bus. They peer down her T-shirt as she leans over the table. They joke with her and I see her teeth laugh and only then do I recognise her, for she has dyed her hair red.

And then she sees me and comes to kiss me on both cheeks. For a blurred instant I smell her hair and I want to bury my face in it. I want to feel her breasts squash against my ribs and hold her against me until the bar melts away and leaves us on the edge of the sea again.

But she draws away and says:

– You chose a good time to come. There's a party tonight, so you'll meet my friends. We'll have a good time and catch up on everything. Oh is that for me? How sweet.

And as she leans over the bar to fill an empty Carlsberg bottle with water from a tap, her skirt comes up high. She drops the rose in the bottle.

– Now don't you dare run away like you did from the army.

And when I most want her to belong to my imagination and to one sublime day in Cape Town, she belongs to the fan-eddied smoke that dims the bar, to the undertones of lust in the jaunty jazz chords, to the leering men. Did I imagine her nipples in my mouth, the nodes of her spine under my fingers?

She swings back to serving tables while I watch from my barstool with the rose in the beer bottle. The men give me dirty looks. But whenever she smiles at me, however fleetingly, she chases the doubts away. Her smile says: You see, the sea is full of fish but you're still my beach boy.

# catch-22

We get a lift to the party with a girl called Sanne (forgetting the red rose on the bar) and the girls chat in Danish in the front. The language is full of vowels strung together and I wish I had learned some Danish from Lars. All I know in Danish is how to order a beer, and I'd been too scared to try it out on the panther girl. And I know how to say I love you. But the chance of uttering those words is fading fast.

At the party I am introduced to Jens and Lars and Bo and other tall blond vikings who cluster at the kitchen window to smoke grass. It is hard to keep Zelda in sight for she flits flirtatiously and elusively from cluster to cluster. My heart reels out after her as she kites away on the gust of a whim.

Once she comes back to draw me towards another cluster of Danes outside the toilet door, gathered there because the beer is chilled in the bath. I don't catch the names but I think they are also called Jens and Lars and Bo. They want to know my feelings on apartheid and injustice and Nelson Mandela. Their questions are prefaced by: As a white African, how do you feel?

I can hear a man peeing as I reel off the words:

– I am not like the white South Africans you see on the BBC, in films. I condemn it.

But all I truly feel, as a circus freak, the white monkey, is every nerve and fibre under my skin wanting to kiss Zelda.

⁂

In the end, when the beer and the grass have gone to my head, Zelda comes back and takes my hand.

– Let's go.

We go along the Gammel Strand, the old fish harbour. The sea wind gusts the blurry fuzz of the grass out of my head. At Nyhavn, Zelda buys us Underground ice-cream in tubs. And we walk all along the deserted harbourside to the mermaid's rock, ice-cream melting on our tongues. I dare not mouth my hopes of tasting her lips and her skin again.

The tide comes in and islands the mermaid from the land. We sit there on the railing together while the moon dances on the sea, the same vanilla moon you can see from a farm at the far edge of the Atlantic, when the blood-orange sun goes down.

– I only have a visa for a fortnight. Then I don't know where to go. If I go back to South Africa the police will pick me up at the airport. If I go back to England, the customsmen may not give me another tourist visa. I'm in a catch-22.

– Shhh, whispers Zelda. Worry tomorrow. For now you're with me.

It is true. I am with the girl I love.

– I read your poems, Zelda whispers.

Then she tilts her face so I can kiss her. Her mouth is humid, her feral tongue forays deep into me, telling me she is no dream.

Then, as if awakened by the far windy whisper of a Zulu sangoma's murmuring over scattered bones and cowrie shells, the mermaid slides from her rock into the sea. She heads out of the harbour, bound south for Cape Town to ferry Nelson Mandela across the shark-finned bay.

6 000 miles south one lone soul, a flapping scarecrow of a man, walks the long road from Paarl to Franschhoek. All day long he walks, guiding a Firestone tyre with two criss-crossed poles. As he walks, he mutters rumours of blood. It is hard to tell if the raggedy man is coloured, or white gone dark under the sun. Maybe the day will come when no one bothers if he is one or the other.

He walks under azure skies. He walks when snow lies on the Franschhoek mountains. He walks all day, until the sun goes down, blood orange, behind the Simonsberg.